DEADLY BARGAIN

Jessie lay swaying as the wagon rumbled along, smiling provocatively up at Pocker leering over her. "You promise you'll let me go?"

"Sure, sure, it's a deal." Pocker broadened his grin. "O' course, I gotta check out your part o' the deal first." He hooked a finger in the low-cut nape of her filmy chemise.

Jessie struck. While Pocker was momentarily distracted, with her left hand Jessie unsheathed his knife and pushed the blade up into his heart. The point struck bone, slid by; the blade went in up to the handle.

Pocker uttered a horrible gurgling sound, then his shoulders struck the floor.

Jessie snatched up Pocker's gun. "Stop the wagon!"

* * *

SPECIAL PREVIEW!
Turn to the back of this book for a special excerpt from the next exciting western by Giles Tippette...

Dead Man's Poker

...**The riveting story of a former outlaw's biggest gamble, by America's new star of the classic western.
Available now from Jove Books!**

DON'T MISS THESE
ALL-ACTION WESTERN SERIES
FROM THE BERKLEY PUBLISHING GROUP

***THE GUNSMITH** by J. R. Roberts*
   Clint Adams was a legend among lawmen, outlaws, and ladies. They called him . . . the Gunsmith.

***LONGARM** by Tabor Evans*
   The popular long-running series about U.S. Deputy Marshal Long—his life, his loves, his fight for justice.

***LONE STAR** by Wesley Ellis*
   The blazing adventures of Jessica Starbuck and the martial arts master, Ki. Over eight million copies in print.

***SLOCUM** by Jake Logan*
   Today's longest-running action western. John Slocum rides a deadly trail of hot blood and cold steel.

WESLEY ELLIS

LONE STAR
AND THE CHICAGO SHOWDOWN

JOVE BOOKS, NEW YORK

If you purchased this book without a cover you should be aware that this book is stolen property. It was reported as "unsold and destroyed" to the publisher and neither the author nor the publisher has received any payment for this "stripped book."

LONE STAR AND THE CHICAGO SHOWDOWN

A Jove Book / published by arrangement with
the author

PRINTING HISTORY
Jove edition / February 1993

All rights reserved.
Copyright © 1993 by Jove Publications, Inc.
Excerpt from *Dead Man's Poker* copyright © 1993 by Giles Tippette.
This book may not be reproduced in whole
or in part, by mimeograph or any other means,
without permission. For information address:
The Berkley Publishing Group, 200 Madison Avenue,
New York, New York 10016.

ISBN: 0-515-11044-2

Jove Books are published by The Berkley Publishing Group,
200 Madison Avenue, New York, New York 10016.
The name "JOVE" and the "J" logo
are trademarks belonging to Jove Publications, Inc.

PRINTED IN THE UNITED STATES OF AMERICA

10 9 8 7 6 5 4 3 2 1

Chapter 1

Through the brief shower of a late-summer afternoon, the Chicago & Alton train chugged northeasterly toward Chicago. Since Joliet, some time before, the train had been flanking the Chicago River, easing around gullies and toiling up brushy slopes, dawdling at the riverbank hamlets of Lockport and Lemon, just as it had at every tank town along the route.

As swiftly as the rain had begun, it tapered to a drizzle and then ceased altogether, scudding west with growly thunderclouds and flashes of heat lightning. Returning sunlight burnished with warming rays the C&A's ten-car bobtail haul of flats, boxes, and coaches. The steam of evaporating rainwater made the muddied expanses dance weirdly, when viewed through a coach's blown-glass windows.

"Chicago!" an elderly conductor called, entering the coach where Jessie Starbuck and her companion, Ki, were seated. "Nex' stop, Chi-cago!"

"High time," Ki groused, and he rose and stretched his cramped legs. "By the schedule, we'll be arriving four hours late."

"And'll be getting off foul with dust, soot, and sweat," Jessie added wearily, stuffing papers she'd been reviewing back in their manila folder. "Before any freshening up, though, we really should speak with Harold Whitworth and learn all the details about this problem."

"This problem" had been growing for a while, threatening physically as well as financially the well-being of Jessie's large packinghouse operation in Chicago—Starbuck Purveyors. There had been increasing attempts at strong-arm extortion and labor racketeering, all of them so far rebuffed by Starbuck Purveyor's general manager, Harold Whitworth. Of course Whitworth had been keeping Jessie informed of how things were going, continually assuring her that he could handle the trouble. Until now, she had not been overly worried. She'd known Whitworth for years, and prized him as an extremely able, honest, and conservative manager.

However, Whitworth's conservatism was why, when his latest report reached her in St. Louis, Jessie had decided to take the C&A and travel to Chicago. Whitworth had informed her, first, that a certain Judge Marvin Nichol had wanted him to join a group called the Civic Reform Council; second, that he had joined, figuring that united they could stand but divided they'd fall against the crooks; third, that the council was suspicious of District Attorney Lewis Emerson, whom the commission itself had gotten elected on a reform ticket; and fourth, that he, Whitworth, had been recruited to help investigate Emerson quietly, by asking a friendly bank officer about Emerson's account—apparently Starbuck Purveyors and Emerson both banked at the same branch of Illinois National.

It wasn't that Jessie necessarily disagreed with Whitworth's actions. It was that when it came to mixing reformers, politicos, and criminals, seemingly simple situations could quickly turn twisty and nasty as a barrelful of rattlesnakes. Quiet, conservative Whitworth had no experience in such matters and might well get in over his head without realizing it. And then it would be too late.

Thirsty and bored, Ki sauntered up the aisle, eyeing the passengers as he moved to join the porter at the watercooler. The coach carried a large quota of gentry, but there were also a number of tinhorns and stock promoters and fortune seekers, and quite a few just plain common folk. Or so Ki estimated. In turn the passengers surveyed him again, just as they had since he and Jessie had boarded that morning.

All the way along, men had been admiring Jessie. In her mid-twenties, she was heiress to the immense Starbuck business empire founded by her late father, Alex Starbuck. Her stylish lightweight wool ensemble was of a tailor-made fit that effectively, if modestly, displayed her full-breasted, taut-thighed figure; and her leghorn hat was perched at a jaunty angle atop soft coils of her long coppery-blond hair. Pert-nosed and full-mouthed, her cameo-shaped face exuded an inner core of warmth and passion and courage, and there was more than a hint of feline audacity in her greenish-golden eyes. But at the moment she also reflected her grave determination to meet and beat this latest challenge. That was why she discreetly carried her custom .38 Colt pistol in her jacket and a two-shot derringer tucked in her dainty chatelaine purse. A lady could never be too careful.

Women cast intrigued glances at Ki. Born of a Japanese woman wedded to an American, he was a handsome blend of both races—tall, bronze-complected, with straight blue-black hair, a strong-boned face, and almond eyes of a dark and vital intensity. Clad as

3

he was in a brown twill suit, collarless shirt, and ropesoled slippers, Ki did not seem much of anything—certainly not a threat, not a man to be reckoned with. Yet, orphaned as a boy in Japan, he had trained in martial arts and the deadly skills of the samurai; and while even now, in his early thirties, he refused to pack a firearm, his suit vest contained short daggers and other small throwing weapons, including the sharp, star-shaped steel disks known as *shuriken*. When, years earlier, he'd first come to America, he'd placed his talents in the service of Alex Starbuck. Indeed, he and Jessie had virtually grown up together, and after her father's murder, it proved fitting for he and Jessie to continue together, as affectionately bonded as any blood brother and sister could be.

At the watercooler, the porter smiled at Ki and shifted to the other side of the vestibule door, which was open on its catch rod. Ki stepped to fill the paper cup with water, and could now see that there were two men swaying on the open platform of the coach ahead.

One was a towheaded lout, sunburnt and peeling, with an S&W Schofoeld .44, grips turned forward for a right-hand draw, under the waistband of his trousers on the left side. The second was thinner and perhaps a decade older, with a sallow, pitted face. A *very* sawed-off shotgun, of a style some fancied for brush work, was thonged with its double barrels downward under his thigh-length buffalo vest. Otherwise the two men were wearing nondescript range garb, and Ki's initial impression was that they were ranch or farm hands, outside taking air.

He was just tilting his head to drink from the cup when a third man came out on the next coach's platform. Ki had an instant's shadowed glimpse of a long-limbed body, a hatchet face, a beak of a nose, and a mouth—which opened with a snarl as the man spotted Ki. He pivoted sideways, his long, dexterous fingers drawing a Colt revolver.

The porter was in the line of fire, but that wasn't stopping the man. "Down!" Ki cautioned, and swept the porter to the floor with his left forearm, as he sprang away from the watercooler, his right hand darting into his vest pocket for a *shuriken*.

Bullets shattered the cooler's glass bottle and gouged splinters from the woodwork above Ki when, crouching, he snapped off the *shuriken*. Somewhere in the coach a woman screamed, then he heard the *thwack!* as his spinning steel disk buried itself in solid bone. He hurled another, choking off the man's strangling cry as he staggered against the railing, then flopped backward on the platform.

Even before the man had landed, a rapid hail of lead from the towhead's pistol was tunneling through the vestibule doorway. Ki flattened out, willing to wait for the erratic salvo to click empty, and wary of the second man's as-yet-unfired scattergun. A drummer close behind Ki was nailed and toppled with a low moan, just as the shooting ceased.

Then a coach door slammed. Ki peered up cautiously. He couldn't see anyone on the other platform now, but he was just thinking he could hear running boots farther ahead when wails and shouts from his coach drowned them out. Four passengers, including Jessie, started toward him, and the porter scrambled for the emergency cord.

Ki yelled, "Stay there!" and sprinted out, vaulting from one platform railing across the coupling to the other, and dropping beside the dead body. It lay staring sightlessly, a *shuriken* sunk in the bridge of the nose and another slicing tangentially through the base of the neck.

5

Ki paused, listening. But there was more noise than ever, the passengers from his own coach disregarding his order, and the passengers from this forward coach equally alarmed, both groups trying to crowd onto the platforms while talking all at once. From the engine a long whistle was sounding, and iron was squealing as brakes locked on.

The train shuddered in a spark-flaring slide, almost tripping Ki as he stepped toward the door. He wanted those two men. He wanted to find them, to stop them before they seized hostages or could jump from the gradually slowing train. Then, abruptly, on his left, a man bellowed out a window. A pistol cracked from trackside, and glass shattered. Ki dashed to the platform steps, grasping the handrail to brace himself against the coach's swaying pitch. Faintly he heard what sounded like scraping feet on the cinders. He clung for a moment, undecided, then swung from the handrail in a quick, twisting dive.

And gunfire erupted. Bullets plowed into wood paneling and rang against ironwork, pursuing Ki to the cinder bed with the hasty aim of a shootist caught unawares. Immediately Ki rolled under the coach, hearing behind him a peevish voice:

"Leave him be, Tyler, we gotta git!"

Ki squirmed fast across rails and ties, while carefully gauging the train's slackening speed. Crawling out on the other side, mere inches from the bladed flange of the wheel, he slewed up and into a crouching run toward the front of the now barely moving coach.

"Here, Max!" From around the back of the last coach, the towhead suddenly appeared at a lope. "The bastard's over here!"

Already the pistol was bucking in the towhead's fist, a swath of slugs drilling the cinders and ricocheting off the car trucks. Ki flung himself at a headlong angle beneath the coach again, cursing silently—that oaf was more persistent than accurate, but he was a fast shot, and had to be one of the fastest reloaders Ki had ever encountered.

Squirreling onto his back and catching hold of a crosspiece, Ki lifted himself clear of the trackbed, letting the undercarriage carry him along. The towhead, kneeling, fired twice more at him. Metal sang with the slugs' impact—just as a pair of boots hurried past Ki. It had to be Max, the scattergun artist. Dropping, Ki quickly slid from the bed and out over the rail, then began snaking up behind him.

"Tyler, I'll go without you!" Max was threatening, angrily brandishing his scattergun at the passengers in the windows. "I will, dammit! I ain't stayin'—" As if he sensed someone coming at his back, he suddenly spun, whirling, and leveled his scattergun.

Ki responded in a blur of motion. One driving step, two steps, and he clamped Max's triggering hand in a merciless vise of steely fingers. Max, reacting with swift savagery, looped a left-fisted roundhouse swing, while yanking his scattergun closer to knee Ki in the groin. But Ki turned a half-pace sideways, dodging the knee as he blocked the swing with his forearm, then wrapping his free hand around Max's right elbow joint.

Guided by Ki, Max jerked up his scattergun and punched its twin muzzles brutally into his own throat—the most vunerable spot, Ki believed, when it was necessary to temporarily silence and disable someone. Such as now. And the iron force of the barrels, crushing against his larynx, muted and stunned Max with paralyzing agony, and the scattergun slipped from his numb fingers, Ki taking possession of it with his left hand while shifting to chop Max unconscious with a *shuto* blow—

"He's mine! Get away!"

Ki swiveled around as Max had, fast, bringing the scattergun to bear. The towhead was trotting from behind the last coach again, nimbly inserting fresh rounds into his hinged-open revolver—a tempting target, but perhaps a bit too distant. Ki checked his impatience, leery of an unfamiliar weapon that was cut specially for spread instead of range.

"I've divvies on this scalp's bounty! Take caution, Max, I don't want to wing you!" That very instant the towhead snapped shut the cylinder, and Max be damned, the lead flew sizzling as he charged.

A bullet buzzed past Ki's cheek, and he figured the towhead had come far enough. He triggered one barrel and felt the jarring recoil of black powder erupting fire and buckshot and gray smoke. A tortured shrieking arose, but Ki kept his finger on the scattergun's other trigger until the smoke dissipated sufficiently for him to see. The towhead was curled over, his arms hugging his belly as though he were sick to his stomach—which he was, there being a gaping crater and shredded meat where his abdomen should have been.

Immediately Ki triggered the other barrel to put the towhead out of his misery. There was no discharge. The hammer fell on an empty chamber or a defective shell.

He turned, then, back to Max. Max was gone. Hurriedly, Ki scanned the flanking underbrush, saw nothing, knew he'd heard nothing, and doubted that Max had had time to cross the trackbed's wide shoulder, particularly considering how dazed and weak and in pain from his injured throat he was. That left the train, which was finally easing to a full halt.

Hastening alongside, Ki surveyed the three coaches, their mostly closed windows crowded with faces. The porters were evidently keeping tight rein on their alarmed and curious passengers, though; the vestibule doors were shut, and nobody was out riding on the platform decks.

"Stay inside!" Ki called up. "Stay inside. There's still one on the prowl or hiding here. Did anyone see which way he went?"

The faces nodded and shook their heads, declaring and gesturing in every conceivable direction. Just goes to prove, Ki thought sourly, the reliability of eyewitnesses. He'd deal with Max on his own.

He slowed, cradling the scattergun. It was useless to him, but he was unwilling to dump it someplace where Max might get it; Max might also have extra shells. Gliding as quietly as a shadow, his free hand always hovering by his vest, he began examining under and between the coaches, working toward the freight cars and engine, frequently glancing behind himself.

The only person in sight was the towhead, now mercifully dead. His pistol was also in plain sight. Ki, having checked it early on, found it warped by buckshot, but left it as bait. He didn't think Max would be lured into the open by so bald a trick, yet he felt it was worth a try. He was more concerned that with the train stopped, Max could readily pass back and forth among the cars. He was near the baggage car, contemplating a climb to its roof deck for an overview, when he detected the sound of a coach vestibule door opening and closing.

Ki dipped down between the baggage car and the first boxcar.

Jessie peered out from the front platform of the last coach, pistol in hand. Her other hand was empty, indicating she'd left her purse with the derringer back inside. After a pause, she dropped to the cinders, then started rearward. Ki swung after her, but had taken perhaps six paces when he saw that she was being stalked. Max seemed to rise out of nowhere, though Ki suspected he'd glimpsed Jessie from the other side and speedily crossed at the coupling.

"Jessie!" Ki tore into a run, tossing the scattergun aside, his own weapons impractical until he got closer. *"Jessie!"*

She heard him and wheeled. Max loomed over her, one hand clutching at her and the other rubbing his sore throat. Jessie backpedaled hastily and leveled her pistol. She fired, but Max spoiled her aim with a lunging, long-armed slap to her gun wrist, and her shot whistled by him. Before she could fire again, he seized her arm and twisted her around.

With Jessie now thrust between him and Max, Ki didn't dare risk using his weapons. But making Jessie his shield was not Max's intention; he wanted her pistol. Frantically he groped and mauled her, wrenching her about as she resisted gamely, struggling in his frenzied grip.

Ki reached Max just as he was swinging Jessie from her feet. Ki's hand bit into the deep muscle crowning the ridge of Max's shoulder—a cruel, implacable bite of fingers, crippling in their savagery. Max released Jessie in his struggle to strike back at Ki. Ki turned him, spearing a stiff-fingered *yonhon-nukite* blow into his belly to bend him, and coldly chopped him into the cinders underfoot with the edge of a hand behind the ear.

Max huddled on one knee, head down, gasping. Ki nudged him with a foot, not gently. "Talk," he said tersely. "Who're you guys after? Me and Miss Starbuck? Who hired you? And why?"

Max grumbled an indistinct answer.

Ki glanced at Jessie; she countered with a light smile. She had stepped back against the coach and was watching silently, tapping the revolver softly yet irritably in her palm, but otherwise not betraying any agitation beyond the tense rise and fall of her breasts.

Ki nudged Max again. "Talk."

Max gave a growly whimper this time. And because Max had been beaten twice within minutes and was abjectly crouching now, Ki was careless for an instant. As Ki's attention briefly flicked toward Jessie again, Max surged upright, flinging a handful of cinders in Ki's eyes. His hand kept on moving, sweeping out and snatching the pistol from Jessie's palm. Then he launched into a wild backward run to gain space, leveling the pistol.

By then Ki was knuckling his eyes and cursing his folly. And Jessie was fit to swear too, for she could have shot Max as he backpedaled—if she'd brought her derringer. "Down! Down quick!"

Ki would not go down. Instead he took Jessie high on the arm with his left hand and forced her downward, while with his right he whipped throwing daggers out from inside his vest, three of them, one at a time, still fighting the pain in his eyes. His vision was blurred, but he threw well, because he could make out Max's form, and the gunman was no longer what Ki considered human. Twice he'd given him the benefit of the doubt and spared his life, but matters were past that now, and Max was just a target.

Max fired, and if he felt anything about killing these two, it seemed to be joy. Ki's first throw and Max's gunshot occurred almost simultaneously, but Ki's blade was already buried in Max's heart when the gunman pulled the trigger, so the shot went wide, whining off into the clear air.

Max stepped back, dying a half pace, and Ki nailed him with the second and third knives as insurance. Max came apart at the seams, collapsing across the roadbed shoulder, faceup, one arm stretched out, with Jessie's pistol lying in his open palm like a gift.

"Thanks, Ki," Jessie said shakily. "Now I'll see if I can remove that grit from your eyes."

She probed delicately at Ki's eyes with a lace handkerchief and brought him instant relief. Ki went over to Max, retrieved his knives, and searched the killer's clothes. Other than a ticket stub showing that the man had boarded at Lemon, he didn't find anything, not so much as an extra shell for the scattergun, which at least explained why Max had been so stingy about firing the thing earlier.

Returning Jessie's pistol to her, Ki climbed up to the platform deck where the first man still sprawled. Again he found a Lemon ticket stub. Otherwise this body didn't yield any clues to its identity, either, although from the watch pocket of the man's denim trousers, Ki dug out a red pressboard token, like a poker chip, good for one free drink at the Dew Drop Inn in Lemon.

Evidently the three killers had gotten on at Lemon, the previous stop—and the last stop before Chicago. Mighty damn coincidental, to Ki's way of thinking.

He was just completing his examination of the dead man when the vestibule door swung open, framing the pale faces of the conductor and the coach porter. The conductor was middle-aged and scrawny, but he puffed himself up like a bantam rooster in a henhouse.

"The Chicago and Alton Railroad don't allow no shooting on its rolling stock and properties," he announced. "You're party to serious offenses."

"Not so fast," Ki said. "I don't carry a firearm."

The conductor scowled and brought a black notebook out of his uniform pocket. "How'msoever, they was shootin' at you. Why?"

Ki was forming a starchy response to that when Jessie stepped up onto the platform, pinned the conductor with a frigid eye, and said, "It is blatantly obvious to anyone with a brain that this gentleman foiled a train

12

robbery. And single-handedly, I might add. The Chicago and Alton did nothing to intercede, and in fact the only action the Chicago and Alton seems to have taken is to permit the bandits on. Is this the way your clumsy railroad always operates?"

"We, er, ah . . . have strict reg'lations, ma'am. Strict reg'lations and requirements, I assure you." The conductor scribbled distractedly in his book, while behind him the porter secretly grinned. "I'm afeared we'll have to notify the proper authorities in Chicago," he continued apologetically. "Just a formality, I assure you, but where there's killings involved—"

"Yes, yes," Jessie cut in wearily. "If we should ever arrive there. We must be stopping at every gopher hole along the line."

The conductor beat a hasty retreat after that, but having been left with no place to vent his own irritation, he chewed into the porter as they left. "Intolerable, Ralph. This laxness must cease. We must maintain prompt schedules and reg'lar stops, y'hear? Now, you and Sam, and Wiley too, fetch them bodies to the baggage car, on the double . . ."

Shortly after the train was under way again, it made another brief unscheduled stop, this time at a lonely telegraph relay station. When Jessie asked, the porter explained that the conductor was having a message dispatched to the authorities. So, when the train finally arrived at Chicago's Union Station, she and Ki were not surprised to see a coroner's mule-drawn hearse waiting to remove the corpses from the baggage car, and a uniformed policeman standing by to take charge of Ki as soon as he alighted. Accompanied by Jessie, the policeman escorted Ki across to two men in business suits.

The fact that the two were wearing suits was their only similarity.

One was a barrel-chested man with gray-streaked hair and a salt-and-pepper handlebar mustache. He was frowning, his eyes the color of suet, his clothes droopy and speckled with food, his sagging vest pinned with a tarnished gold badge marked Chicago Police. "Chief Felix Weims," he said, introducing himself.

The other man Jessie had met once before. He was Phillip Bolanger, the assistant manager at Starbuck Purveyors. Imposingly tall and broad-shouldered, he had a patrician-nosed face with a firm mouth, bulldog jaw, and piercing hazel eyes. His hair was a thick, dark brown, with just a hint of gray at the temples to make him look distinguished, but not old. She estimated his age as about forty. He wore a cutaway suit of dark silk-mixed cashmere, an immaculate white shirt and a carefully knotted string tie, and supple black boots on somewhat smallish feet. And if Jessie hadn't been looking for it—and known how to look for it—she could have easily missed the small-caliber pistol in a shoulder holster, concealed by his suit jacket.

Bolanger looked worried and sounded a bit distracted as he greeted them. "A pleasure to see you again, Miss Starbuck, and you, Ki. I'm sorry we must meet under such tragic circumstances."

"Please call me Jessie, if I may call you Phillip," Jessie replied, trying to set him at ease. "And thank you for your concern. But really, you shouldn't have bothered. There's no evidence that the gunmen had anything to do with us directly or with Starbuck Purveyors."

"Oh, that's not why I'm here, Miss—Jessie." Bolanger licked his lips. "No, I felt it my duty to be the first to inform you of the other news."

"Other news?"

"I . . . I'm afraid Mr. Whitworth is dead."
"Dead!"
"Yes. He was shot down this morning, on the way to work."

Chapter 2

There was an old Oriental belief that a man's vices concerned nobody but himself—and, maybe, the Devil. But anyone who subscribed to the vice of killing a Starbuck employee was beyond the pale. And if—*when*—he was tracked down and caught, he was apt to be invited to meet the Devil pronto, no questions asked. Or so Ki was thinking as he stared at the porcelain operating table. Brilliant white gaslight brought Harold Whitworth into sharp relief lying there, the surgeon's hands casting shadows on the corpse's lower chest and abdomen as he probed for the death-dealing bullets.

Outside the gaslight's radiance stood Ki, Chief Weims, and District Attorney Lew Emerson, motionless, not speaking, watchful not only of the surgeon but of each other. Except for the metallic snick of the instruments, it was very quiet in the room. Ki had the impulse to break things with his hands.

One by one the surgeon extracted three bullets and dropped them into a shallow porcelain tray. "There you are," he said, and drew the coarse sheet up over Whitworth's face.

Ki said, "How about letting Mrs. Whitworth see him now?"

"Sure," Weims said, and nodded at the surgeon. The surgeon folded the sheet down neatly and closed Whitworth's eyes, then began washing his hands in a basin of fresh water.

District Attorney Emerson moved forward then and picked up one of the lead pellets in the tray. Ki judged him to be about his own age, perhaps a few years older, perhaps a little too handsome for his own good, with a cleft chin, a straight thin nose, and eyes that were dark and hard. "You don't need 'em all, Chief. My office oughta have at least one, right?"

Chief Weims chuckled harshly. "Afraid we'll lose 'em?"

"Stranger things have happened," Emerson said.

Weims spread his hands. "You can't rile me, Lew, you know better'n that." He turned to the surgeon. "See that he gets one, labeled all neat and nice. When you get the coroner's okay, send the others over to the department for identification."

"I'll take mine now," Emerson said, examining the one he had chosen. "No need to wait for department ID, either. A .45, I reckon, and by the five grooves twisting to the right, it's from a Smith and Wesson. No offense to you and your experts, Chief." He obviously didn't care how offensive he was to the police department.

For a moment the tension in the room was terrific. Then Chief Weims shrugged and went out the door to the anteroom, to collect Mrs. Whitworth. He returned with her in tow; she was sobbing, quietly, as though she had something to be ashamed of. Accompanying her was Jessie, her expression somber, impassive, betraying none of the emotions broiling beneath the surface. In concordance with Jessie, Ki looked stoic, his eyes and lean features concealing his actual mood behind a mask of outward dispassion.

Inwardly they both seethed. Harold Whitworth had been shot down on the street in broad daylight, leaving behind a bride of less than a year, Millicent. She was a diminutive young woman whose oval face was white and drawn, with dark circles under her eyes, but on the whole she seemed to be standing up under the strain pretty well. The girl might have been plain, Jessie thought, but she had character, something to be admired in anyone. Certainly Harold had had character. Being shot down like a mad dog was too bad an end for such a brave, loyal employee. Well, loyalty breeds loyalty, and somehow Starbuck would repay Harold Whitworth his full due.

Weims cleared his throat. "Now, p'r'aps one of you could tell me what Whitworth was involved in."

Jessie affected surprise. "Involved in? Mr. Whitworth was general manager of Starbuck Purveyors, and devoted himself strictly to business."

Weims blew disgustedly through his lips.

Jessie's face hardened. "You listen here. I'd tell you who killed him if I knew, but I don't." Shadowed by her hat, her eyes considered the district attorney; she wondered if Emerson had taken care of Whitworth personally, or if he had farmed the job out. She thought she had better have a little heart-to-heart chat with this Civic Reform Council, especially with Judge Nichol.

"Trouble with you rich Western ranchers," Weims said in an aggrieved tone, "you always think city cops don't want to solve, uh, crimes like this." He became earnest. "How the blazes can we if important folks like you won't back us?"

"I'm always glad to cooperate with the authorities."

"But you don't know nothing, ma'am, is that it?"

"What's there to know? Mr. Whitworth was in charge of carrying the payroll. From what I've heard of this sweet town of yours, that'd be incentive enough."

Chief Weims sighed. "We get all kinds, for a fact." Clearly he was a man who refused to be insulted.

Emerson spoke up: "Miss Starbuck, I'd appreciate you dropping by my office in the morning."

"I'll try, but I've Mrs. Whitworth to consider, y'know."

"I'd like to ask her a few questions, too. Just routine."

"Very well."

Weims said, "We got enough trouble in Chicago without any cowboy feudin' going on." Short thick legs carried him to the door. "Better let the police handle it, Miz Starbuck."

Jessie gave him a tight-lipped smile. "Is that a suggestion or an order?"

Hand on the knob, Weims paused. "Don't get me wrong, ma'am. I don't mind your askin' around a little, just so you come to me if you find out anything. Just so you come to me *first*." He went out.

The surgeon followed him. District Attorney Emerson gave Jessie, Ki, and Millicent each a brief, neutral nod, then he too went out. The sudden vacating of the room made Jessie conscious of Harold Whitworth there on the table. She put an arm around the widow's shoulder.

"I'm sorry, Millicent, truly sorry."

"Yes," Millicent said. After a while she said, "He was the only man who ever bothered to give me a second look. I'm going to be awful . . . empty without him."

A short while later, after Millicent had left for her home, Jessie and Ki departed the morgue's examination room in the Cook County Hospital and rode off in their livery buggy. Ki handled the reins of the one-horse, green Brewster two-seater, which Jessie had rented from their hotel stable. They headed out of the main business section, toward the stockyards, crossing the

Chicago River and driving along blocks of small shops, boardinghouses, and tenements. Although some places were grimy and delapidated, most were kept up and showed pride of ownership. The Great Fire of 1871 had destroyed much of the city, but the disaster had actually opened the way for new advancement, the wooden buildings that were swept away by the flames replaced by more substantial structures of brick and stone.

Presently they approached the extensive railroad switching yards that served the Union Stockyards. Opened in December of 1865, the Union Stockyards provided for the livestock industry facilities far superior to those that had hitherto been afforded by the smaller, scattered yards. The meat-packing industry, too, had been going through a process of rapid consolidation that was resulting in the disappearance of many small firms and the appearance of such great establishments as Armour & Company, Libby, McNeill & Libby—and Starbuck Purveyors. Starbuck had begun long-distance shipping of refrigerated meat in the late 1860s, and the processing of meat byproducts by Starbuck and the other large firms was developing into an important adjunct of the packing industry. The packinghouses were noted for converting "everything but the squeal" into usable products. The squeal—and the smell. The odor of animal flesh, alive and dead, was pervasive over the stockyards. As a result, the packinghouse firms put their office headquarters near enough to their operations for control, but far enough away to avoid most of the stench.

The Starbuck office was in a yellow brick building sandwiched between two produce houses. It was a compact, pugnacious sort of a vault, one-story, with a raised loading platform of concrete and an arched, corrugated iron roof. "Starbuck Purveyors," the sign above the open overhead door read. So did the lettering etched in the frosted glass of the front entrance door. Ki parked the buggy by the entrance, tethering the bay to the boardwalk tie rack and, with Jessie, started walking toward the platform dock.

Standing on the dock, talking to an employee, was Assistant Manager Phil Bolanger. Jessie had told him to take over as acting manager, and as yet she saw no reason not to appoint Bolanger permanently as general manager. Now, stepping down from the door to meet them on the boardwalk, Bolanger politely doffed his hat and said, "Welcome to Starbuck Purveyors, Miss Star—Jessie. I've made all the company records and files available for your perusal."

"Thanks for your effort, Phil, but the accounts can wait. I'm sure they're in order," she replied. "We didn't have a chance before to talk candidly, without certain official ears overhearing us. So right now I'd prefer hearing about the criminal element that had been threatening Harold."

"Not Mr. Whitworth personally—threatening all of us, as Starbuck Enterprises," Bolanger said, frowning. "Candidly, this town is shot through with crooks. We've tried to clean them up, but they've got men planted in strategic posts. Right now I'd hazard the Garibaldi family is probably our biggest threat, at least directly. Ruben 'The Gimp' Garibaldi and his four sons, all of 'em tough as a boot. The Gimp is reputed to've made his fortune from labor slugging and racketeering, if'n you know what I mean."

Jessie nodded. Back at the Starbuck headquarters on her Circle Star Ranch in Texas, she had read reports estimating that the Chicago labor force had reached almost half a million workers. Faced with the problem of making their way in a changing economy, and restive under the hardships of their lot, workmen had been seeking to better their condition by organization.

Chicago had become one of the focal points of the developing labor movements, suffering periodic outbreaks of labor violence such as the rioting connected with the great railroad strikes of 1877. The city was ripe for exploitation by criminals bent on shakedown and protection rackets.

"The Garibaldis supplement their earnings," Bolanger continued, "with the proceeds of frequent safe robberies, payroll holdups, and even highway robbery. At least two of The Gimp's exploits are noteworthy even for this town. He led his crew of gunmen into West Side railroad yards and stole a hundred thousand dollars' worth of pelts and furs from a string of freight cars; and year before last he carried out the famous robbery of the Old Crow warehouse, wagoning out almost two thousand barrels of bonded whiskey and leaving in their stead as many barrels of water. He was indicted for this, together with ten of his gang, four city detectives, and officials of the warehouse company, but no one was convicted."

"And his sons?"

"Ben Garibaldi is the oldest and is in his mid-forties now. Then comes Al, three years younger. After Al is Pete, a couple of years younger. And a year younger than Pete is Nate. After he was born, Ma Garibaldi, wearied of bearing sons for ol' Ruben, lay down and died, so it's claimed. As soon as each son got old enough, Ruben staked him to a part of the Garibaldi territory. The Gimp's Old Lompoc House saloon has been their combined headquarters, and for all practical purposes, they control the entire West Side here. It ain't enough, of course; never is. They keep shoving their boundaries outwards on all sides, crowding crook and honest man alike."

"And they've been pressuring us?"

"You betcha. As you know, that's what prompted Mr. Whitworth to join the Civic Reform Council, not that it seems to've done much good. Folks opposing the Garibaldis keep getting kidnapped right off the streets, never heard of again. Or murdered, like Whitworth. Some of 'em even get framed and sent to prison."

While they were talking, a black-bearded man in rumpled garb approached along the boardwalk. A few feet behind him, out in the street, a canvas-sided freight wagon was trundling along, drawn by four mean-looking black Spanish mules. Jessie gave them no more than a peripheral glance as they passed the building, finding nothing to distinguish them from the other pedestrians and street traffic.

The sudden fireworks started as the bearded man was striding by Phillip Bolanger. The man suddenly lunged forward, giving Bolanger a fierce push that sent him stumbling to his hands and knees. Now a pistol was flashing sunlight along its barrel as it started up in the man's hand for the quick kill.

To her dying day Jessie would never see anything else like it. Ki seemed to spurt throwing daggers from his vest, three sharp blades embedding themselves in the man's torso, at heart level, bringing him down in a tumbling heap. Before the man hit ground, Bolanger had his own pistol in action and was killing a tall, blond fellow who had swung around on the seat of the wagon only to come pitching down with a bullet through his head.

Those mean Spanish mules must have saved all their lives. There were four more men in the wagon, but they had been a split second slow in taking their part in the fight. The canvas side wall was coming up as if something had gone wrong with it at the last instant, and revolvers and shotguns were ready to let go when the mules lunged. The men inside the wagon were jerked off their feet. Like a white cloud of destruction on the move, the wagon plunged down the street with Phil Bolanger firing at it.

It was a stampeding calamity for the length of the street. The stout front hub of the wagon caught the rear wheels of a buckboard. There was a splintering crash, broken wood, and iron tires flying and the rear end of the buckboard coming down in the dust like some queer beetle. Then the two mustangs hitched to the buckboard and tied to the hitchrack flung themselves back and took off after the rumbling and swaying wagon.

Mules brayed, horses bawled. The wagon sideswiped a fine surrey; the surrey went over, spilling its occupants as its team ripped loose and galloped after the mustangs and the crazy mules. In another moment it looked as if the whole block were being taken apart. Then the dust hid it all, leaving only the roar, the crashing of more wood, and the sound of people shouting and cursing at the tops of their voices.

"My God," Jessie gasped breathlessly. "What was that all about?"

"A ride-by shooting," Bolanger answered, remarkably calm considering their narrow escape. "A Garibaldi trademark," he added, standing up.

"First the attempt on our lives on the train," Jessie said grimly, "now this. Garibaldi, Emerson, *somebody* sure wants us dead and gone."

It was Ki who responded. "Well, you can't prove it by this gent." He was kneeling beside the dead bearded man, checking his pockets. "No identification, not that you'd expect any." Straightening, he said grimly, "This is just like an ambush, only moving instead of hiding. Were they after us again, Jessie, or after you, Phil?"

Reloading his pistol, Bolanger shrugged. "Perhaps all of us."

"I wish I knew why . . . ," Jessie said, gazing down the street at the dust cloud dissipating in the wagon's aftermath. "And I intend to find out, before they strike again. Phil, a social call to the Old Lompoc House might well be in order. Is it a gents only barroom, or can ladies go in, too?"

"Oh, it's quite respectable, and I doubt we'd be in danger on the premises," Bolanger answered. "The Garibaldis like their operations to look respectable. The cops stage raids and make arrests—but only where The Gimp says. If we go to the Old Lompoc House this evening, we shouldn't get into any trouble."

I wonder, Jessie thought as she turned back to Bolanger, who was brushing himself off with a large handkerchief.

"Wouldn't you care to retire to the office?" he asked affably, donning his hat. Then, smiling, he extended his arm for Jessie to take and walked with her toward the front door without so much as a glance at the dead men he was leaving behind him.

Chapter 3

Later, on toward evening, Ki drove Jessie to the mansion of Judge Marvin Nichol. While he waited outside in the buggy, Jessie went up the front steps and tugged on the bell cord. A stout, middle-aged housekeeper ushered her inside, along a parquet-floored hallway, into the library of the home. It contained large couches and lounging chairs done in tan glove leather and formally arranged around a fireplace, over which hung a pair of crossed cavalry pennants. There were oil portraits on the walls, which otherwise were lined with bookshelves, and sprays of flowers on the tables, marble statues in the corners, and drawn brocatelle drapes over the windows. The library showed elegance, and bespoke money.

Already present were three men, the executive committee of the Civic Reform Council. They failed to impress Jessie much. Apparently she didn't evoke much enthusiasm from them, either, for there was an air of watchfulness in the way they accepted her accusation that they were directly responsible for Harold Whitworth's murder. She stood with her back to the fireplace and surveyed her host and the other two guests without affection.

"You gentlemen don't know what you're doing," she said. "The proof of that is lying on a table in the morgue." She turned her critical stare directly on Judge Nichol. "You asked Harold Whitworth for his help. You set him up to nose into the affairs of a district attorney you elected but apparently couldn't trust. Just a quiet little investigation, you told him, no danger at all. So he agreed to something with his eyes closed. He never had a chance to defend himself."

Seated behind his desk, Judge Nichol grew red and stiffened in his chair. No longer active on the bench, he was white-haired, bejowled, and a little flabby with age, yet strength and stubbornness still etched his blunt features, and indignation now showed on his wrinkled face. "Young lady," he said, "isn't it possible that you're jumping to conclusions? The Garibaldi clan was trying to intimidate Starbuck Purveyors through your Mr. Whitworth, that's what brought him to our group. He was the object of a simple if brutal lesson."

From the depths of a leather club chair came a sigh. Jessie felt that Mr. Thurlow Dobbs was not addicted to sighing, that this was just an emergency sigh. She felt that here was a jovial teller of tales who'd give you the shirt off his back. He was a fat pink cherub literally overflowing with the milk of human kindness. He was president of Lincoln State Bank & Trust Company. "You better not let Ruben Garibaldi hear you talking like that, Marvin. You're liable to end up in a mortuary."

"Besides, Marvin, if you're making a list, you might add the brunette," the third man said—a fellow named Ichabod Temple, who Jessie would've sworn was an undertaker, though it turned out he was Chicago's leading real estate broker. "The brunette seems to have nothing to do and a lot of time to do it in."

The connection escaped Jessie, but apparently hit home with the judge. The color deepened in his cheeks. "I wouldn't pursue that line of thought too persistently either, Ike. Cyrene Yarbrough is a friend of mine."

"Sure she is," Thurlow Dobbs said with a fat chuckle. "I've seen you out with her plenty of times."

"Thurlow," Nichol growled, "don't give Miss Starbuck the impression we're taking this lightly."

"My God," Dobbs said. He appealed to Jessie. "I'm in this council for twenty-five grand. Does that strike you I'm taking it lightly?" His triple chins quivered indignantly.

Jessie had never heard a bank president refer to thousands of dollars in terms of grands before, but then she had never met a realtor who looked like a mortician either. She asked, "How are the Garibaldis involved?"

"Up to their ears, that's how." Ike Temple sounded bitter. "Ask anybody. Ask the newsboy on the nearest corner. Gimp Garibaldi and his boys are the men behind the gun, and if they haven't got Alderman Churlak and Chief Weims—yes, and now Lewis Emerson, our eminent young district attorney—in their pocket, I'll cast my vote for all of 'em at the next election."

"Well, as I understand it, you elected yourselves a district attorney," Jessie said, "and don't think you've gotten your money's worth. Obviously you must have some reason to suspect Emerson of crossing you."

"Suppose we don't care to divulge our reasons?" Dobbs said.

"That could only mean," Jessie said evenly, "that you yourselves are convinced Emerson killed Whitworth, or had it done, but you aren't going to do anything about it." She turned toward the door. "Very well, I'll go to the opposition with what I've got."

Judge Nichol came to his feet. "Now wait a minute, Miss Starbuck." For the first time a vestige of genuine emotion touched his bleak face. "If the boy is guilty, he'll have to be punished. None of us is arguing that." He drew a slow breath. "Here's something that perhaps Whitworth didn't tell you: Lewis Emerson is my son-in-law."

"And the father of his grandchild," Ichabod Temple said. His voice was tipped with acid. "Naturally a public exposure would be most, uh, distasteful to him."

"To all of us, for that matter," Dobbs said in a gently chiding tone. He addressed Jessie. "Nobody likes to be made to look like a sucker. That's what happens if the man we ourselves elected turns out to be a stinker. We promised the voters a new deal. They haven't been getting it."

"If anything, convictions have been fewer and farther between than they were under the former incumbent, who admittedly took his orders from the Alderman Churlak faction. Emerson says it's because of lack of evidence furnished him by the police department." Temple cracked the knuckles of his bony hand. "So far there's nothing against Emerson but intangibles. What got us suspicious, aside from his general evasiveness, was when he pulled his account out of Thurlow's bank and took it over to Illinois National."

"You ask him about that?"

"Could we?" Dobbs demanded plaintively. "Without letting him know that we suspected he was as crooked as a dog's hind leg?"

"He must've given you some kind of excuse."

Dobbs nodded. "Oh, he did. He and I had a nice little quarrel over the handling of some of his investments."

"You check with Illinois National?"

"Illinois National isn't a local institution," Dobbs replied, shrugging. "It's a branch of a chain out of Springfield, the state capital, and they don't want any part of our local politics."

"I suppose you told Whitworth about this?"

"Yes," Judge Nichol said in a curiously lifeless voice. "I want you to know how deeply we all regret Whitworth's death, Miss Starbuck. On the other hand you must see how utterly unpredictable it was. We didn't want him to tackle known sources of corruption or vice, just to confidentially ask around. If it turned out that Emerson was honest, and he discovered what we'd been doing, he would be irreparably hurt. Yet if he'd actually sold us out, we had to get rid of him, you see?"

"Yes, I see," Jessie said. And she did; away from the look in Millicent Whitworth's eyes, she could view the case a little more objectively. It was obvious that whether or not Whitworth's killing was directly attributable to District Attorney Emerson, it must surely have stemmed from the council's investigation. It was possible indeed that while asking about Emerson, Whitworth had accidently learned facts inimical to someone else—to, say, Ruben Garibaldi. Had Whitworth in turn been identified with the council's activities, his elimination would have followed almost as a matter of course. Jessie considered broadcasting that she was throwing all of Starbuck's power and influence behind the council, thereby stirring up greater public support—maybe. It certainly would stir up the killers to greater and swifter action, though, and she doubted that would be to her or anyone's advantage. When the time came for the showdown, she wanted it to be at *her* time, on *her* terms.

Judge Nichol glared at his guests. "I'd like to be sure that whatever's been said in this room won't go any farther."

"I'd like to be sure of it, too," Jessie said. "Then I'd know where to look in case anything happened to me." Her smile was only slightly sardonic. "Anything less permanent, that is, than what happened to Mr. Whitworth."

After Jessie departed, and was riding away with Ki, she discovered that someone was following their buggy. She glimpsed a rather paunchy horseman riding a gray gelding a short distance behind. The rider seemed to be paying attention to everything in sight but them, and that raised her suspicions.

"Maybe I'm just edgy after that attempt at the office, Ki, but I don't like the looks of the rider in back of us."

Ki glanced behind. "He's no beauty, but I've seen uglier."

"That's not what I mean. I think he's tailing us."

"Well, let's find out." Ki turned the buggy into a side lane and kept the bay at an even, unhurried walk through a series of alleys and back streets. Behind them came the rider, the gap between them neither lessening nor widening.

"He worries me," Jessie said. "I think we should find out who the man is, Ki. I'm pretty sure he didn't follow us to the judge's, which means the judge must be under more or less constant surveillance."

"You're right," Ki said. "Let's take him down the garden path, shall we?" He pulled over, got out of the buggy, and wrapped the reins around a convenient picket fence. Then he and Jessie crossed the street, walking somewhat rapidly, but not enough to give the impression that they knew they were being tailed. They never did know how the guy dismounted and tagged after them as quickly as he did; all they were sure of was that he was behind, making an occasional footfall out of step with their own.

Reaching a corner, they paused, as though uncertain of their way, and finally turned left. This street was a shadowy tunnel of trees, and skirting one side a tall hedge extended along the grounds of the corner house clear down to a mid-block alley.

"This is as good a place as any," Jessie said.

Abruptly they ran, their feet making staccato sounds on the hardpan street bed, echoing in the dusky stillness. As abruptly, they stopped, and the sound faded away into nothingness. They withdrew quietly into the sanctuary of the tall hedge. Brambles scratched their noses, and Jessie had the impulse to sneeze. By breathing deeply through her nose, she managed not to.

Presently they were conscious that, almost beside them, a man was standing, seemingly glued to the trunk of a live oak. They held their breath for what seemed like five minutes before the man moved away from his tree, trying to make himself part of the hedge. In his right hand he was holding a short-barreled revolver.

Reaching out with his left hand, Ki grasped the man's gun wrist in an *atemi* hold, which caused him to drop the revolver, and whipped the man around to face him at the same time. The rock-hard heel of Ki's left hand shot forward and smashed the man squarely between the eyes. As the unconscious man started to fall, Ki simply embraced him and pulled him through the hedge, to lay him peacefully on the ground.

"Anyone around?" he asked Jessie.

She shook her head. "I don't hear anything. Is he all right?"

"Yeah. He'll have the king of all headaches tomorrow, though."

Swiftly Ki ransacked the man's clothing, handing what he uncovered to Jessie. They were not too surprised to find a police badge pinned to a wallet, in which there were seven dollars, some assorted cards, and a letter written in purple ink by a woman who signed herself "Babe." The rest of the man's personal effects were commonplace.

Ki retrieved the man's fallen revolver—a Harrington & Richardson Police Special—and put it back in its shoulder holster. He replaced the other effects, including the wallet and money, just as he'd found them—all except for the badge, which he'd unpinned from the wallet and now pinned carefully to the front of the man's pants, like a fig leaf.

On their way back to the buggy, Jessie remarked, "I wonder why the police department is so interested in Judge Nichol's callers."

Ki shrugged, then grinned wolfishly. "I wonder if our detective back there will know me, if he ever sees me again. I hope not . . ."

Returning to the main street, they headed south into a middle-class neighborhood filled with squat, square houses, some brick, some frame with stone foundations. All sat close to the walkways. Ki stopped the buggy at a two-story foursquare cottage whose trellised front porch edged the street line.

When Millicent Whitworth answered their knock, they saw with some surprise that she was still fully dressed; indeed, she had on her hat and coat. She stood aside to let them in. The living room was small but neat and comfortable, and there was a door open to a bedroom beyond.

"Thinking of going out?" Jessie asked, not caring for the look in the young widow's eyes. They were feverish, excited, and doing their best not to show it. It occurred to her that Millicent was a potential loose cannon, perhaps even a menace.

"What if I was?" Millicent's tone was defiant. "I've tried to rest, to sleep. I couldn't." In her hands a beaded chamois bag bulged a trifle more than it should have.

"I'm sorry I had to leave you alone so long, Millicent."

"That's all right." She dropped her bag on a sofa and took off her coat. She did not take off her hat.

"There's something I wanted to ask you," Jessie continued, her eyes tenderly sympathetic. "Did Harold tell you what he was up to?"

"He said they were having trouble with the district attorney."

"Nothing more?"

Her "No" was a little too quick, a little too positive.

Jessie nodded. "It's always hard for amateurs to lie well, Millicent. It takes practice, lots of practice, and a sly mind." She picked up the bag, weighed it thoughtfully. "Give me three guesses as to what you were intending to do."

The widow closed her eyes and swayed a little. "I wasn't!"

"Sure you were," Jessie said cheerfully. "Harold was looking into the affairs of a man named Emerson when he was killed." She opened the bag and took out a .21 hammerless pistol. "So you were going to even the score by shooting Emerson." She put the pistol in her purse, along with her own derringer. "I'm not saying you're wrong, Millicent—about Emerson. I just don't think you'd know how to go about getting away with it." She sat her on the sofa, gently. "You don't have to worry about the payoff, Millicent."

Millicent began to cry, not noisily. When her sobbing finally subsided, Jessie gave her a handkerchief. "All right, blow your nose."

Obediently Millicent blew her nose. "I . . . I guess I just got jittery, waiting." She shivered, though it was not cold in the room. "Waiting and thinking."

Jessie nodded, not entirely convinced, however, that Millicent wasn't holding out on her. "Listen to me. If I was smart enough to guess Harold told you something, you think somebody else won't? You think you can go running around Chicago without getting hit by the same thing that hit your husband?"

"Does it make any difference what happens to me—now?"

"Does it make a difference?" Jessie was outraged. "How can I convince you that I need your help?"

That got her. "Help? How?"

Jessie was almost taken off guard by Millicent's ready acceptance of the idea. She pretended to be thinking deeply. "Well, for one thing, there's something that smells about the Emerson angle. Not that I've given up," she hastened to add, "but after talking to some of the local talent this evening, I'm not sure enough to go throwing lead at him, or to let you do it." She sat on the sofa, next to Millicent. "Come on, take a load off your mind. Maybe you can make me sure."

"Well ...," Millicent hesitated. "All right, Harold did say something more, just once." A little color came into her cheeks. "We had planned a kind of celebration, you see. I'd just found out there was going to be an addition to the Whitworth family."

Jessie's stomach tied itself in a hard knot. She exchanged meaningful glances with Ki, thinking, If we needed anything else, this is it. She carefully refrained from saying anything.

Millicent's voice remained flat, emotionless, but her hands were tearing Jessie's handkerchief. "Harold didn't tell me very much, really. Just that Emerson seemed to be running around with some funny people, for a reform candidate, and for a supposedly happily married man."

Jessie remembered Ike Temple's allusion to a brunette, a brunette who seemed to have nothing to do and a lot of time to do it in. Cyrene Yarbrough. "He mention any names?"

"He said he'd run across the boss of a crime family."

"Ruben Garibaldi?"

Millicent nodded. "Yes, that was it."

"But you weren't going to look up Garibaldi," Jessie said. "You were gunning for Lewis Emerson."

Millicent stood up abruptly. "You wouldn't understand this, but if I'd needed anything else it was the way Mr. Emerson looked at me, there at the morgue." Her eyes were feverish again.

"Millicent!" Jessie said sharply.

Her shoulders lifted in an almost imperceptible shrug. "Oh, I'm not going to do anything." She gave Jessie a brief, forced smile. "I can't very well now, can I? You've disarmed me."

Jessie cursed inwardly. "That's just the point. Now that I think about it, you ought to have a gun—for your own protection. I wasn't joking when I said you might have visitors." She got to her feet, began striding around the room. "Look, if I give it back to you—"

Millicent shook her head. "No, you better keep it, Miss Starbuck—Jessie." Her laugh held a hint of hysteria. "We pregnant women can't be trusted, you know." Her mouth twisted. "Or so I've heard. Personally I've never been pregnant before." She lay down on the sofa, facedown. "Good night, Jessie. You too, Ki."

★

Chapter 4

The Metropole Hotel was ever so slightly off the beaten path, a block from Michigan Avenue in downtown Chicago. The interior was elegant, with terra-cotta floors, gray stone columns, and vaulted ceilings; the rooms spacious and well-furnished. In Jessie's sixth-floor room, the gas jets were lit and the drapes were pulled, although the window behind the drapes was open, allowing the busy nighttime sounds to filter in from the street.

Jessie paced back and forth restlessly. It seemed to her that, unlike that brunette she had now heard about twice, she had a lot of things to do and very little time to do them in. She thought it was funny that people should first point her to District Attorney Emerson, and then, as though by deliberate intent to confuse, point her away from the man. In Emerson's favor were two things: first, the exhibited antagonism between him and Chief Weims; second, the fact that the police were watching Judge Nichol's house. Nichol was not only Emerson's father-in-law, but head of the council committee that had hired Emerson. Yes, the distrust evinced by Emerson and Weims could have been an act put on for Jessie's benefit. But if so, that would mean they both knew what Harold Whitworth was up to and were working in cahoots. And she couldn't judge that on the basis of one meeting.

Jessie was more sure of how things were between Chief Weims and Judge Nichol. The police stakeout on Nichol's home proved that Weims was, if nothing else, a man of foresight. He knew about the council, knew that it was gunning for him, and he intended to be prepared for any eventuality. Thinking of the stakeout reminded Jessie that she herself was in a somewhat precarious spot. However, she thought it unlikely that the cop could swear it had been Ki, in the company of Jessie, who had struck him down; indeed, it was unlikely that he could actually identify her as one of those who had visited Judge Nichol.

Jessie placed Millicent's pistol under her clothing in one of the bureau drawers. She felt that while this was not particularly ingenious, it would at least keep the young widow from finding it, should the mood for vengence again overcome her. The police or other interested parties could find it and be damned. She was rearranging her clothes in the drawer when there was a knock on the hall door. Her late caller turned out to be Chief Felix Weims.

"So you finally got back" was the chief's opening remark. He was not exactly affable. Down the corridor at the next door—the door to Ki's adjoining room—lurked a second man, obviously a detective, though not the one Ki had waylaid.

Jessie was relieved. "What do you mean, finally? Am I supposed to report my comings and goings to you?"

"No use getting snooty about it," Weims said. He came in, closed the door, and put his broad back against it. "I've been hearing things about you, ma'am."

Jessie was intrigued. "What sort of things?"

"Unladylike." He wagged his head sadly, like a parent whose offspring has brought home a bad report card. "You wouldn't be the first dame that took a gent's killing as a personal affront." He sighed. "Even us cops like to pay off for our own." He began moving about the room, heavily, seemingly without aim. "Sure, I checked on the famous Miz Starbuck from Texas. In my place, wouldn't you like to know what's going on in your own bailiwick?" He saw, or seemed to think he saw, that he was making some headway. "You see? I'm leveling with you, ma'am. Why can't you come clean with me?"

"What makes you think I haven't?"

The chief's already florid countenance turned an angry magenta. "To he—heck with this double-talk." He pointed a blunt forefinger at Jessie's chest. "I've been trying to be fair with you. Now I'll put it this way: You try pulling any fast ones, you come in here and set this city on its ear, I'll throw you and your bodyguard in the can so quick it'll make your heads swim." He stormed out, slamming the door behind him.

Jessie made a face at the quivering door panel, thinking angrily that she had no reason to trust Chief Weims any farther than she could throw city hall. She was not at all sure that for reasons of his own the chief hadn't had Whitworth killed himself. Especially after Ichabod Temple's asserted belief that Ruben Garibaldi had the chief in his pocket, and Millicent's confession that Whitworth had told her he'd run across Garibaldi's name in his investigating.

Fifteen minutes later, she knocked on Ki's door. When he answered, she said, "I think it's about time we paid a social call on Ruben Garibaldi and his clan."

Garibaldi's Old Lompoc House turned out to be a better than average club housed in a freshly painted two-story brick building. Light glowed through a facade of frosted glass windows. The interior, they found, was noisy and smoky. Its brick walls were painted a dull red, and at the near end, up three shallow steps, was a supper room. Perhaps twenty or thirty tables surrounded a small but not cramped dance floor. The three-piece band was playing a waltz, and the soft *shush-shush* of dancing feet had the sound of lazy surf on a coral beach. At the far end was the saloon section, with black-tie bartenders pouring at the thronged, mirror-blazing bar.

The patrons were a mingle of ages and types, mostly rich folk and the spoiled brats of rich folk in fancy dress. Also in tuxedos, Jessie and Ki noticed as they took an empty table, were quite a few brawny gentlemen whose faces and hands indicated very physical occupations. Like breaking bones.

Jessie was surprised to see Lewis Emerson at a table. She had thought the district attorney would be burning the midnight oil, in an attempt to circumvent the alleged trickery of the police department in the matter of such things as the bullets taken out of Harold Whitworth's body. She looked at Emerson's companion and was no longer surprised. The lady was dressed in a black satin gown, and against skin that was as white and evenly textured as fine percale, her mouth was a scarlet slash, and her eyes a deep azure blue. But it was her hair that really drew attention; it was of a lustrous chestnut brown and swathed her head in great looping coils. Jessie could well imagine that when it was unpinned and allowed to fall, it was long enough to literally reach bottom.

Jessie leaned toward Ki. "What do you think?"

"Of her?" Ki exhaled noisily. "All I ask is to be buried in the same cemetery."

Behind them, a voice spoke up: "That can be arranged."

"Perhaps I best settle for an introduction," Ki said, turning with Jessie to look at their companion.

"That might be arranged, too," the man replied, and nodded to Jessie. "G'evenin'. Welcome to my joint, Miz Starbuck." Ruben "The Gimp" Garibaldi was tall and raw-boned and hawk-beaked and lantern-jawed; his eyes were like wet marbles, and his grizzled hair had been the color of new rope when he was young. Now it was grizzled gray and balding.

"Who made it their business to tell you who I am?" Jessie demanded, less than friendly.

Garibaldi shrugged. "How should I know? Weims or Emerson or somebody. Is it supposed to be a secret?" Around his paunch was a burgundy cummerbund; it was agitated, giving rise to the suspicion that the man might be chuckling. No sound came from his lips, nor did his face change. "No secrets up here, Miz Starbuck. The city and the state's wide open." Then he said quietly, "They tell me an employee of yours ran into a little tough luck a coupla days ago."

Jessie's face was wooden. "That's why I'm up here."

"Any ideas?"

"No."

"Maybe I can help you," Garibaldi said. "I've done pretty well up here. I'll have my boys take the cotton out of their ears."

"That's mighty nice of you, Mr. Garibaldi," Jessie said.

"Forget it."

From some point beyond Jessie and Ki's range of vision a woman had come into the dining area. She had on a green-checked mackintosh over what appeared to be a house wrapper, but it was not this that held them. It was the frozen sleepwalker's look on her dead-white face. Her eyes were burning coals, and in her right hand she held a pistol. Jessie didn't need more than three guesses to convince her that this was Emerson's wife—she looked much like her father, Judge Nichol.

At Jessie's side a cricket began an insistent chirping. She discovered that the cricket was a tiny silver whistle between Garibaldi's lips. Garibaldi himself had not moved.

Two men rose from tables on opposite sides of the dance floor, to head off the woman with the gun. Here again family resemblance helped Jessie and Ki make identifications. The two men had to be sons of Ruben Garibaldi. Which two they couldn't tell, but there was no mistaking the Garibaldi nose and the Garibaldi jaw and the Garibaldi eyes, and something of the old man's toughness.

Ruben Garibaldi took hold of Ki's elbow. "I'll introduce you to the brunette, pal. Excuse us, Miz Starbuck."

Jessie reckoned it would not have done much good to protest, but in truth she had no objections. The brunette played a role in this, of that she was certain. The precise nature of the role was another matter, and she doubted the brunette would admit much of anything to another woman. If something were to be found out, it would have to fall to Ki to find it.

Ki and Garibaldi hastened toward the table with Emerson and the brunette. So did the gun-toting woman, but by now the two men had closed in on her and had her arms. Even at that she almost got away from them. Emerson turned, half-rose; his chair fell over but made no noise against the background of music from the now-frantic band. Ki and Garibaldi tried to hide the subsequent scene from the dining area behind them.

"Get her out of here," Garibaldi said to Emerson. And to the brunette, "You, Cyrene, stay where you are."

The two men wrestling with Emerson's wife couldn't get her to release the pistol. Somehow, reflexively, she managed to trigger it, making a hell of a racket in spite of the band. Like an echo, there was the smack of a fist against flesh and bone.

Even as she sagged, her husband, now becoming a hero of vengeance, hit the Garibaldi son who had done it a full-armed blow in the mouth. Even the band was surprised into silence. In the hushed aftermath Emerson's voice came clear and distinct:

"I'll take care of her." Quite without hurry he bent and untangled his unconscious wife from the even more unconscious man. He picked her up and, carrying her as easily as though she were a child, stalked out. Ruben Garibaldi and his other son assisted the man from the floor.

Ki looked down into a pair of azure eyes. "Garibaldi was going to introduce us," he said. Against the bronze of his skin his teeth shone whitely. "I guess he kind of forgot."

"Then we'll just have to do without Garibaldi," Cyrene Yarbrough said. Her voice was an organ alto. "Will you buy me a drink, please?"

One drink led to another.

And they led to her home.

The Yarbrough home was a frame bungalow, smaller than the Whitworth house but more plushly furnished. The front room contained a three-piece, overstuffed and tassled Turkish parlor suite. The bedroom, which Cyrene insisted on showing to Ki, boasted an enameled and brass "marriage"-size bedstead. Ki looked at the bed, then at Cyrene, then around the room.

"Yours?"

"Just leased for the season," she answered, closing the bedroom door.

"Why, Cyrene," he said in mock surprise as she moved closer, "are you suggesting I stay the night here?"

"Is that so awful?" she murmured, scrutinizing him with her luminous green eyes. Her chin was raised, and her uptilted face was yearning. "I admire strong men, and you were so brave back there at the Lompoc."

"Ma'am, it doesn't take much spunk to talk to Garibaldi."

"I mean Opal," she said. "Opal Emerson. She's a notorious hussy."

"She seemed to me intent on keeping her husband, even if it killed him," Ki replied, wondering what the devil Cyrene was dancing up to. "I bet Mrs. Emerson is deep down underneath as prim and proper as a maiden aunt."

Cyrene didn't believe him. "She leads men astray. She'll turn your head if she can, and I need your help." Cyrene inched closer, her eyes wide with concern. "You can find things out. Have you already? What little tidbits of talk did you hear?"

"Nothing in particular."

"Are you sure? You can trust me."

"I'm positive."

"But you'll try, for me?" she pleaded. "I'll pay."

"Why, Cyrene, are you offering me a bribe to spy?"

"What's so bad if it brings a killer to justice?" She eased still nearer, intimacy creeping into her voice. "And I'd be grateful, personally very grateful," she coaxed, touching his arm, her red mouth curving in a bewitching smile. "I might be persuaded to raise my price, even change it to something you might like better . . ."

Ki smiled. "Would you, now."

"I've been very lonely, living here," she mewed, stroking his shirt with her fingertips. "And the men are all so dull."

"Strange, I haven't found it dull in Chicago so far."

"It is, if you're a woman," she said with a pout. "My friends are all married with one or two fat babies, and someday it'll be the same for me. Oh, I've had my chances, but I don't want to marry any city fellows. They're all accountants and office boys, while a Western outdoorsy man like you . . ."

Ki was growing aroused, but he was also growing tired of playing her game. He wondered how far he could get with her, or rather, how far she'd go for what she wanted of him. She was now so close he could feel her warm breath against his face, but greedy as she might have been, she evidently wanted him to make the initial pass. So Ki slid his hand over her shoulder and kissed her. She responded with enthusiasm, the pressure of her body like an eager promise.

He began to fondle one of her breasts. "Some folks might think, Cyrene, that you were trying to turn my head."

"I'd never hope to lead the likes of you astray," she sighed, wriggling some. She didn't object or become angry when he started fondling both her breasts, seeming to resign herself to an adventure right then and there. In a minute or two, moaning softly, she fell, embraced with Ki, across her bed. Her dress hiked up to her knees when she lay back, but instead of adjusting it, she crossed her arms behind her head and stared up at Ki.

Ki didn't wait for a formal invitation. But as soon as he had her shoes off and was fumbling with her belt, she stopped him.

"Leave my clothes on," she said.

"What the hell?" Ki said.

She rubbed the leg nearest to him against his leg, and pulled her hem up a little. She had nice legs, long and not too muscular.

"You're wrinkling my dress." Changing her mind about the belt, she unhooked it herself, then pulled her dress up around her hips and spread it out under her back. "You guys are all the same," she said, as Ki moved to her lace-trimmed pantaloons. "All you ever care about is getting a girl in the sack."

"What's wrong with that? You like it, don't you?"

"Let's not discuss it."

"Now you're being sensible."

Her drawers were a tight fit, and the drawstring dug into her belly. Putting her hands behind her head again, she arched her buttocks off the bed to help Ki tug the drawers down and off. "How'd you know I'd be willing?" she asked.

"I don't know," Ki said, dropping her drawers to the floor. And he didn't. How could any man know anything about a woman?

In any case, his vague answer seemed to satisfy Cyrene. "Now you," she said. "You're not going to keep your suit on, are you?"

"Don't go away." Ki stood and started shedding his clothes.

Cyrene watched him strip with that vacant, burnt expression some women got when they were ready for sex. She was breathing hard, as though there weren't enough air in the room, when, naked, Ki climbed back on the bed and knelt over her.

"I'm taking off your dress and things," he told her, "like it or not."

Even while Cyrene was shaking her head no, Ki undid her dress and yanked it free. Tossing it on top of her pantaloons, he rolled up her undervest to bare her firm, round breasts, and then he stretched out close alongside her, gliding his hand down over the smoothness of her body to her buttocks. They were elegantly shaped, and her breasts were warm and taut against his chest. She raised her face and pressed her open mouth tightly against his, her hand searching down between the two of them. He couldn't help gasping as the tease of her fingers closed around him, and he ground his pelvis into her, pulling her beneath him. She opened her legs to accept him, and he plunged deep into her soft flesh.

"This is nice," she sighed, straining back against him.

Ki thought it was pretty good, too. He could feel her body throb as she undulated her hips against him, her thighs pressing against his legs as her ankles snaked over and locked around his calves.

"This is nice," she repeated shakily. "You helping me . . . in every way. I know you'll find out what's happening, I know it."

"For God's sake, if you keep thinking about Emerson or what-all, you'll miss what's happening now."

"I'm not missing a thing," she said, clenching him tighter with her arms and legs. "But I can't help thinking how we'll finally be able to rid Chicago of thieves and murderers."

Keeping her too busy to talk for the next few minutes, Ki didn't give a damn about thieves and murderers. He didn't give a damn about anything except the exquisite pleasure building explosively within him. He could feel that Cyrene was also nearing completion, as she gripped him tighter and moved more urgently.

"If I'm getting too loose for you," she gasped beneath him, "I can put my legs together. That'll pinch me tighter."

Too late. Ki didn't even have time to tell her never mind, as he climaxed violently up inside her. She shuddered, convulsing, crying out orgasmically. He collapsed limply, and she lay still, pressed firmly around him. When at last he rolled from her, they lay quietly side by side, exhausted, satiated.

Finally Cyrene yawned and rose from the bed. "I have to tinkle." A twinge of self-consciousness stole over her as she took her chamber pot from under the bed and squatted over it. "I don't want you to leave," she said while pissing. "Tell me about living in Texas, working for the famous Miss Starbuck. I've always heard she was—"

"I know. Hard-nosed. A bitch. She's not." His eyes were bright and hard and intent now, watchful as she returned the chamber pot and climbed back on the bed. "But that's all the talking about her or anything I'm doing."

"Talking?" She stroked his bare leg. "What d'you mean?"

He smiled thinly. "Don't give me that. You know why Miss Starbuck is in Chicago. I think everybody in town knows why we're up here."

"Harold Whitworth?"

"Yes."

She leaned forward, put both elbows on the bed and cradled her chin in interlaced fingers. "Ordinarily I don't go around giving people advice, Ki. But if I did, and I were to give you any, I'd suggest that you and Miss Starbuck just forget Whitworth."

"Thanks. I'll think it over."

"Now you're angry."

"No."

They stared at each other for a long moment. Then, eyeing Ki with wary coyness, she cupped his groin tauntingly. "Like I said, stick around a while. Who knows, things might get interesting... if you're up for it."

Ki was up for it...

Next morning, he discovered to his pleasure that she was also a good cook. Fortified by a breakfast of bacon, eggs, toast, and coffee, he left her bungalow and headed back on foot to the Metropole Hotel. When he reached Michigan Avenue, he heard a newsboy yelling his lungs out about the murder.

Thinking that perhaps something new had developed, Ki gave the kid a dime and accepted a press-damp *Chicago News-Dispatch*. Harold Whitworth's killing wasn't even mentioned. The murder the *Dispatch* was featuring today was that of District Attorney Lewis Emerson. Someone had shot him unto death in the— as the *Dispatch* writer put it—"early hours just before dawn."

Ki's face was so stiff it hurt. After what seemed to him a long time, he discovered that his hands had practically shredded the *Dispatch*. He thrust the remnants into a nearby garbage can, then crossed Michigan Avenue diagonally and headed up the next block to his hotel. Win, lose, or draw, his first job was to confer with Jessie.

Entering the Metropole lobby, he ran smack into the arms of Chief Felix Weims.

"Ah," Weims said happily. "Nice morning, ain't it?" Behind him loomed his companion of the night before and another detective—the one Ki had conked. Ki didn't let on he recognized either detective, and put on his sleepy, no-brains-at-all look.

"What's on your mind, Chief?"

"I like that," Weims said. His face was benign, almost jovial. "People calling me by my title, all respectful an' all. You might say . . . well, it does something to me in here." He laid a meaty fist over the region of his heart. "You see the papers yet?"

"Matter of fact, I have."

"That why you were in such a hurry?"

Ki was puzzled. "Why should I be? Emerson doesn't mean anything to me, or to Miss Starbuck."

Employees and guests in the lobby were beginning to stare now. As though appreciative of his audience, Weims thrust out a hairy paw and got a fistful of Ki's suit lapels. "The hell he doesn't mean anything to you! You knocked him off!"

"Me?" Ki felt an overwhelming impulse to put a knee where it would do the chief the most harm. He mastered it. "Whatever gave you that idea?"

"I kinda admire you, Mist' Ki, but we got you on ice." He searched his pockets for a cigar, found one, and stuck it between his liver-colored lips. "Just so's you won't feel too bad about it, though, I'll tell you how it happened we caught up with you so soon. Seems a manager of Miz Starbuck's was checking up on our crusadin' young prosecutor. Seems like the 'cutor didn't like that. So he ups and shoots this Whitworth deader'n a poop. Then Miz Starbuck and you arrive, and on account of Whitworth working for Starbuck, you naturally have to kill Emerson on orders from Miz Starbuck. Of course, we wouldn't have caught the tie-up if this bank officer hadn't come forward and said a man named Whitworth had approached him about the Emerson account."

Ki's smile held just the right amount of triumph without inviting a fist from his nearest captor. "Sorry to disappoint you, Chief, really I am, but the fact is I've got an alibi for the early hours just before dawn. Name and address on request." He leaned forward and breathed in the chief's face. "The lady is going to be very mad at you, though, if you force me to mention her right out in public like this."

A kind of glassiness came into Chief Weims's eyes. His voice was scarcely more than a whisper. "The brunette?"

Nodding, Ki managed to look a trifle smug. "Ask her."

"Don't think we won't," the chief muttered. And then, quite suddenly, he was his old self again. "Okay, we've got even a better bet." He looked at his men. "Let's go and talk to the widder lady."

Ki licked his lips. "Whoa up, Mrs. Whitworth couldn't have—"

"Shaddup," said the detective Ki had clobbered.

Surrounded, Ki was hustled back out of the hotel and around the corner, into a waiting canopy-top wagon. There was a police department logo painted along each side, and a uniformed patrolman handled the reins of the team. With the other detective sitting up front giving directions, they set off at a smart trot in the direction of the Whitworth cottage.

But when they arrived, they found the house deserted. A quick check determined that Millicent's personal effects were missing. Mrs. Whitworth had vanished.

Chapter 5

"Miz Starbuck, I can't tell you how I 'preciate you showin' up at the station like this," Chief Weims said. "I want to be fair with you, and with your boy Ki here." To prove how fair he wanted to be, he had allowed the sap looped to his hairy wrist to leave hardly a mark on Ki's face. Beside Ki's chair stood two detectives, ready to grab his arms in case he showed a disposition to defend himself.

Jessie stood in the doorway, seething with rage, and a little breathless after her rush from the hotel to the police station. The desk clerk who had given her the tip would be well rewarded, she'd see to that. She stepped forward, controlling her fury. Against a window that had not seen water or rag for some time, a fat bluebottle fly buzzed loudly. The chief's sap made smacking sounds against the palm of his hand.

"We was just conversin' with your bodyguard, Miz Starbuck, about who put Mist' Whitworth up to checking on Emerson. P'r'aps you know?"

She ignored the chief. "Are you all right, Ki?"

"Yeah." His lower lip was swollen, but he had all his teeth.

Weims raised his voice. "C'mon, ma'am, there's the officer at the bank."

"I haven't talked to the officer, or anyone else at any bank here. Neither has Ki." Jessie was glad they hadn't. That would've been all Chief Weims needed to convince him they were active accomplices of not only Whitworth, but of Mrs. Whitworth. Upon consideration, though, she put a trip to the Illinois National high on her list of things to do.

"Okay, so maybe you didn't know," Weims conceded, "but Mrs. Whitworth could've known, couldn't she? From her husband?"

"Anything's possible," Jessie hedged. "Don't leave me in suspense, Chief. Did the bank officer tell Mr. Whitworth anything?"

"He says not." It was apparent that the chief had given this angle some thought himself.

"If he wanted to keep his job," Jessie said, "he could hardly say anything else."

"Well, it don't make much difference." Weims sighed. "When we get Whitworth's wife, we'll know all these little things. And don't think we won't get her, ma'am."

Jessie glanced at Ki. "Millicent's missing?"

Ki nodded, briefly relating his trip to the Whitworth home and finding her gone. Then, easing his cramped, rigid position in an armchair that was too narrow for him, he said to the chief, "I'll make you a little bet. I'll bet you don't find her."

"Meaning you know where she's hiding?"

"Meaning I think someone does. Someone who doesn't want her found—ever."

Weims blew out his cheeks. "That's kinda hinting that it wasn't her who shot Emerson." His eyes grew sly.

"I took her gun away from her," Jessie argued.

"And where is this gun now?"

"In the drawer of my bureau, at the hotel."

"We'll see, we'll see. Anyhow, she could've gotten another."

That was something Jessie herself was afraid of. She remembered her last talk with Millicent, and wished she had stayed instead of just taking her gun and leaving. She was not at all sure that the brunette, Cyrene Yarbrough, hadn't picked up Ki last night with the deliberate purpose of insuring that Millicent was defenseless against what could be an elaborate frame-up job.

"Mrs. Whitworth must've had something in mind, or she wouldn't have packed a gun." Weims sounded almost eager. "It's open and shut."

"If you can prove that Emerson killed Whitworth and that Mrs. Whitworth knew it, I'll grant you she's a good suspect."

"Whaddya mean, *a* suspect? You got anyone better?"

"Sure," Jessie said evenly. "You."

Weims yelped as though someone had stuck a pin in him. "Remarks like that get people's teeth kicked in."

"You hated each other," Jessie pressed. "But if you don't like that, I'll give you another one: Mrs. Emerson."

Weims was startled, then stared sourly. "By God, you better lay off thinking along those lines. You know who she is?"

"Judge Nichol's daughter." Jessie smiled mockingly. "I found that out after the ruckus in Garibaldi's." Deliberately she went over and placed a hand under Ki's elbow, urging him to stand. "Anybody happen to mention that brawl to you?"

"I heard," Weims growled, eying Ki darkly. Finally he made a sweeping motion to the two detectives. "You boys wait outside." As an afterthought he added, "And you, Brody, try to keep anybody from cutting your throat while you're not looking." When the door closed, Weims turned to Jessie again. "Now, you were saying, ma'am?"

"I understand that Emerson was shot in his own home. At that time of the morning who could've had a better chance than his wife?" Jessie pretended to inspect her nails. "She was jealous. She had a gun, which is more that you've proven so far against Mrs. Whitworth. At least fifty people saw her with it."

"But she hasn't vamoosed," Weims said significantly.

Jessie sighed. "There's that, isn't there? Still, you might ask her to let you see her gun."

"She claims she lost it."

"How convenient," Jessie said, a mite cattily, and started to walk out of the office with Ki. In her mind was a perfectly clear picture of an austere, rather arrogant gentleman whose daughter had committed a murder; who knew that she had committed it, and who, in order to save her pretty neck, had saddled the job on Millicent Whitworth.

Chief Weims made no effort to detain them.

They returned to the Metropole, where Jessie left Ki off to freshen up. Taking over the reins of the buggy, she drove by herself to the home of the late Lewis Emerson.

Under the watchful eyes of a nurse, a little girl was playing on the lawn of the house—a little girl who apparently didn't know that her father was dead. In the drive a chauffeur in a plum-colored uniform was polishing a black canopy-top surrey. He appeared to be watching the child, but he was really watching the dark-haired nurse. As Jessie went past him, the front door opened and Judge Marvin Nichol came out. The judge's mind seemed to be on something he had been saying to the pert maid in prim black and white behind him, for he did not immediately see Jessie. When he did, he was not pleased.

"What're you doing here?" Then, remembering that both the maid and the chauffeur were within earshot, he turned and looked at the hovering maid. "That'll be all, Gertrude."

Gertrude backed into the hall and closed the door. The chauffeur strolled across the lawn toward the nurse and the playing child. The judge turned angry eyes on Jessie. "Well?"

"I'm going to have a talk with your daughter."

"About what?"

"Last night, for one thing. About what prompted her to make the kind of scene she did."

"You can't. I won't allow it."

"I'll see her, or I'll tell the police and the papers that it was you who talked Whitworth into investigating her husband. How do you think she'll like that?" Even as she spoke, Jessie realized that she might be looking at the murderer instead of the murderer's father. She remembered the not-too-veiled insinuations of Ike Temple; the way Judge Nichol had leapt to Cyrene Yarbrough's defense. She wondered if young Emerson hadn't offered the older man some pretty stiff competition in the quest for the brunette. And she'd heard that when you got to be sixty, you took these affairs of the heart pretty seriously. With that theory as a basis, it was practically no trouble at all to see why Whitworth had been sent nosing after Emerson. It was a roundabout but apparently efficient method of eliminating Emerson. First you killed Whitworth. That would bring—at least it had brought—the Starbuck faction and Whitworth's wife on the scene. Then you knocked off Emerson and blamed it on one or the other, whichever was handier.

Nichol suddenly looked old and tired. "You think my daughter killed her husband?"

"I don't know. I'd like to find out."

"And what do the police think?"

"The police in this city don't seem to do much thinking. At least if they do, they're afraid to put their thoughts into words." Her eyes were unfriendly. "I think the lot of you would be infinitely relieved to just let the whole thing drop, let an outsider like Millicent Whitworth take the charge, and if she's never found, so much the better."

"But you're not going to let the thing drop?"

"Not until I'm convinced Mrs. Whitworth is guilty."

Nichol drew in a slow breath. "So be it, then." He turned and opened the door behind him. "Gertrude? Will you show Miss Starbuck into the parlor, please? And tell my daughter she is to answer her questions." He nodded briefly, without friendliness, to Jessie. "Good day, ma'am." He marched down the steps and toward the adjacent stable. The chauffeur hurried from the nurse to intercept him, a hand holding his cap. The child, too, ran toward her grandfather, and Jessie saw the stiffness go out of the old man's shoulders, and an expression in which there was little but bitterness come into his eyes.

Inside, doors opening off the lower hall disclosed a living room, a dining room, a den. The doors were all open, almost carefully open, as though to create the impression that there was nothing whatever to conceal. Jessie was ushered into a small, comfortable room bright with chintz and flowers, and the sunshine streaming through open casement windows at the south end was golden warm. When Mrs. Opal Emerson came in, Jessie saw that there were only faint shadows under her eyes, in the hollows of her cheeks.

"My father sent word that I was to talk to you."

"Yes, I heard him," Jessie said, and introduced herself. She made her voice gentle, compassionate.

"Believe me, I know what you must be suffering at this time, but it's necessary that a few details be cleared up. There're a few people in Chicago who feel that ... well, that the case against Mrs. Whitworth is a little thin. Perhaps if you were to help me, we could stop all this talk going around."

"Talk?" Mrs. Emerson selected a chair, sat easily, gracefully. "About what?"

"About you." Her eyes, her tone, denied that Jessie herself put any faith in these rumors. "You see, there were quite a few witnesses to that little affair in Old Lompoc House last night. I won't say they have the right to know what happened afterward, but they think they have."

Quite suddenly Mrs. Emerson grew angry. "Haven't they done enough to us? Isn't it enough that my husband is not only dead, but that he's labeled a murderer, a man who couldn't stand investigating?"

"It's quite obvious that you yourself were doing a little investigating, Mrs. Emerson. With a gun. By the way, where is the gun now?"

Fear crept into the woman's face, her voice. "I don't know."

"You told the police you'd lost it. Is that right?"

"It's gone, that's all I know. I mean, someone struck me and I was ... unconscious when Lew brought me home. I suppose the gun may've fallen out on the way home ..." Her voice trailed into nothingness.

"All right," Jessie said, "we'll let the gun slide for the moment." She appeared to weigh her next words carefully. "I imagine this wasn't the first time you'd suspected your husband of cheating." She drew a slow breath. "You were jealous. You wanted him to give up this woman he's running around with, but then you learned he hadn't. And you struck back."

Mrs. Emerson stood up. "You don't believe that!"

"It makes a pretty tight case, as good a case as they've got against Millicent Whitworth."

"Then why haven't they arrested me?"

Jessie shrugged. "Your father's a powerful man in Chicago."

"You mean he's protecting me?"

"Or himself."

That tore it. Mrs. Emerson sat down abruptly, weakly, and buried her face in her hands. Jessie let her cry for a little while, then pressed on, her voice flat, emotionless.

"Your father could've seen what was going on. A proud old jurist like he is wouldn't be apt to let someone walk all over his own daughter."

"He didn't do it, I swear it!" Mrs. Emerson lifted a tear-stained face. "Oh, Father knew things were wrong, more than just Lew's infidelity. Money was getting more and more scarce. Even the servants hadn't been paid for two months. There was only one conclusion to draw, Miss Starbuck."

"Yes. That the woman was milking your husband dry."

"Lew denied it, of course. He'd made some unfortunate investments, he said, and swore that his interest in Cyrene Yarbrough was strictly business. That he was trying to gain evidence."

Jessie was genuinely astonished. She, and probably Harold Whitworth before her, had been working on the theory that the district attorney had moved his bank account because it was being swelled by graft. Now it seemed, to believe Mrs. Emerson, that her husband was actually on the skids.

Jessie asked, "Did your father know all this?"

Mrs. Emerson nodded. "Well, most of it. Father was already displeased with Lew's handling of certain prosecutions. They'd—" She saw her mistake and looked quickly at Jessie to see whether she'd noticed it, too.

Jessie had. "Quarreled?"

"Perhaps a little," Mrs. Emerson admitted.

"But you didn't tell him about your own troubles?"

"No. We Nichols have always liked to think we were just a cut above average; you're not supposed to run sniveling to teacher the first time something slaps you down. You try to work out your own problems."

"Like you did last night, for instance?"

"That was silly, wasn't it?" Mrs. Emerson stood up and crossed to the open windows. Distantly, out on the front lawn, the little girl laughed shrilly. The woman at the windows shivered. "Very silly, when one looks back on it. At the time I suppose I became just a . . . well, just another woman who was losing her man. You see, Lew had promised me he wouldn't see her again."

Jessie had a brief flash of intuition. "Someone tipped you that he'd be found at the club with her?"

"Yes. A messenger delivered a note. It was unsigned." Then Mrs. Emerson said fiercely, "But if you think it was my father, that for reasons of his own he wanted to . . . Miss Starbuck, is that what you're trying to prove?"

Jessie moved toward the door, to leave. "I'm trying to prove that Mrs. Whitworth isn't a murderer. To do that I may have to prove that your husband wasn't either. Think it over, Mrs. Emerson."

Out in the hall Jessie paused, looked back. Mrs. Emerson was still standing there, a grave figure, staring at nothing in particular. Jessie continued on outside without any conspicuous feeling of satisfaction. Crossing the front lawn, she carefully avoided looking at the little girl in the hand-worked pinafore.

When she returned to the hotel, two men were waiting for her in the lobby. One was Ki, dressed in a clean suit. The other had a jowled, double-chinned face that sported a mustache and goatee. He looked smugly satisfied, preening his goatee with a ring-studded hand, nary a ruffle to his elegant clothes—black frock coat, pearl-gray trousers and vest, and a ruby stickpin thrust in his silk stock. Jessie did not recognize him, though his natty attire and a couple of news photographers lurking nearby hinted that the man might be important—somebody, say, like Alderman Churlak.

"Mrs. Starbuck? Vaughn Churlak." The alderman's smile had a lot of teeth in it. He seized and wrung Jessie's hand. "Chief Weims has been telling me things about you."

Jessie glanced at Ki, at his swollen lip, then back at Churlak. "Did he tell you he almost knocked my friend's teeth out?"

Churlak was momentarily saddened. "Felix is impetuous. I often mention it to him." He brightened. "You mustn't bear us any ill will."

The photographers chose this moment to ignite their phosphorescent powder and blind everybody in the lobby. Jessie wondered if Churlak hadn't notified them in advance. It would make a fine picture for the voters to see: the alderman on exceedingly cordial terms with the wealthy Texas employer of Harold Whitworth, husband of the woman accused of murdering the district attorney. She released Churlak's manicured hand with the feeling that she had touched something dirty.

"Well," Churlak said briskly, "I just wanted to make you feel at home in our fair city." On the point of departure, he appeared to think of something. "Oh, you weren't serious about what you told Weims earlier, were you?"

"Mrs. Emerson, you mean?"

"Yes."

"Would it make you very unhappy if I were?"

Churlak sighed. "I always think it's best to let sleeping dogs lie, don't you?"

"You're willing to let the case against Mrs. Whitworth die?"

Churlak closed one eye. "Between you and me, she did the administration a favor. I'd say we wouldn't press the hunt too hard." His eyes lifted suddenly, toward Ki. "Maybe we could accommodate Miss Starbuck to the extent of blaming you for his killing."

"Only I've got an alibi," Ki said.

"And I'd be the last one to suggest she might change her story," Churlak said. He gave Jessie a sidelong glance. "Still, she could." He became once more the dapper politician. "I hope you'll be with us a long time, both of you." With a flourish he bowed, and with another flourish departed.

Jessie looked at Ki, who stood stone-faced. "Don't say it, Ki. I know what you're thinking about him, and don't say it. Let's buy a newspaper."

The noon edition of the *Dispatch* carried a pen-and-ink illustration of the bank officer whom Whitworth had approached for information. His name was Gregory Boothroyd, and the caption referred to him as a public-spirited citizen. Chief Weims gave him full credit for the solution of Emerson's murder, a crime which might otherwise have been very baffling indeed. Neither *Dispatch* nor chief attempted to hazard a guess as to why a packinghouse manager named Whitworth should be interested in the district attorney's bank account. The reader was left to suppose that the facts behind all such minor details would be learned immediately upon the apprehension of Mrs. Whitworth. The whole account had a carefully sympathetic note. There was even a degree of sympathy for the fugitive, and it was hinted that she would be dealt with lightly if she would only come forward and give herself up. As yet she had shown no signs of doing so.

Gregory Boothroyd himself showed signs of fluster as he came out of the side door of the bank. After all, he was currently being lauded as a public-spirited citizen. But there was no band to greet him, no throng of cheering Chicagoans, so looking a bit disappointed now, Boothroyd became just another drop of humanity in the sidewalk tide. Jessie and Ki became two more drops, flowing in behind and then side by side with the man by the middle of the block.

The entryway of an abandoned store offered a degree of privacy. Ki neatly tripped Boothroyd, caught him, and then with every evidence of contrition, forced him into the recess. Ki's back was to the sidewalk; so was Jessie's. Boothroyd's back was pinned to the door of the defunct establishment.

"Now," Ki snarled, "we and you are going to have a talk."

"Wh-what about?" The bank officer looked as though he were going to be sick. "Who are you, anyway?"

"Friends," Jessie said, smiling in a vaguely affable manner. In a sense, she and Ki were bluffing, using the old bad guy–good guy—or in this case, good gal— routine so beloved by cops when interrogating suspects. "You might say we're friends of Harold Whitworth's."

Boothroyd paled. "Let me go or I'll scream for help!"

This was the first time Ki had ever heard anything with pants on say he would scream. "You do, and I'll let you have a couple right in the belly." His fist in his jacket pocket poked the fabric like a gun. "It'll be your last whinny, bucko."

Boothroyd swallowed thickly, evidently believing Ki. "What do you want?"

Jessie nodded. "That's better." Reflected in the glass of the empty display window, passersby appeared incurious about the three of them standing in the doorway. The noon sun was warm on Jessie's back. "Look, Gregory, all we want to know is what you told Harold Whitworth."

"B-but the police, I . . . I already told them I didn't—"

"That's all right," Jessie assured him. "We won't make you out a liar. We won't even tell them that perhaps you had a sneaky little notion of blackmailing Emerson."

"Blackmail!"

"Sure," Ki chimed in, grinning. He released the pressure of his forearm against the smaller man's chest. "When Whitworth was found dead, you had Emerson over the well-known barrel, didn't you?"

"No! No, I didn't know Whitworth was dead until after I'd found out Emerson was, too. Anyway, I'd have known better than to try to get money out of a man who scarcely had a dime to his name." He licked dry lips. "Okay, okay, Whitworth approached me, and as a favor I checked Emerson's account. I was a tad surprised to find that in just three months, the account had dropped from nearly a hundred thousand dollars to nothing. Whitworth was surprised, too."

"Where did the money go?"

"The big withdrawals were all drawn to cash."

"Emerson have a safety deposit box?"

"Not with us."

"All right," Jessie said, "one more question and you can go. Could anyone have known you were interested in Emerson's account and tipped him off? Anybody but you and Whitworth?"

"I don't know. I wasn't looking for anything of the kind, and I'm pretty sure Whitworth wasn't either."

"Thanks, Gregory. Have a nice lunch."

Released, the bank officer scuttled away, out of sight.

"Wonderful," Jessie said disgustedly. "His story confirms what Opal Emerson told me, Ki, and it leads to one conclusion: Someone was bleeding the district attorney dry."

"Meaning Emerson must've had something to conceal. Even if he'd just been squandering his money on the brunette, he wouldn't have wanted it known. So Emerson himself still remains the logical suspect for killing Whitworth, and Millicent the number one selection for Emerson's death."

They allowed the stream of sidewalk traffic to carry them back to the main stem, where presently they located the offices of Ichabod Temple & Associates, Real Estate. It was an elaborate ground-floor suite with an entrance opening off the lobby of an office building, and another off the street. Across the street, Brody, the cop Ki had hit, was pretending an intense interest in a bowl of chrysanthemums in a florist's window. The chrysanthemums looked as artificial as the man's interest. Jessie was momentarily intrigued by the notion of Detective Brody keeping Ike Temple under surveillance. It reminded her of Brody's unfortunate vigil outside Judge Nichol's house the night before.

Inside Temple & Associates, there were a lot of desks but not many people, probably because it was the lunch hour. A prim lady with graying hair and spectacles ushered Jessie and Ki through a ground-glass door in a mahogany-and-glass partition. They found Ike Temple with his feet on a desk. He looked as though he had been asleep.

"Hello," Temple said without enthusiasm.

"Don't be so cordial," Jessie replied. "Anything I hate, it's people fawning over me."

"I haven't got much reason to love you two." Temple took his feet down and pushed a lock of lank black hair out of his eyes. "The council is hardly going to be able to lift its timid head around here after this. Seems our candidate wasn't exactly the type to inspire public confidence."

"Is that my fault?"

"Well, no," Temple conceded. "Still, Whitworth was your boy."

"Which reminds me, who had the idea first to make Whitworth *your* boy—Judge Nichol, Dobbs, or you?"

"Not me. No, I may've needled Nichol a little about his son-in-law, but I didn't think we needed help to tell us there was something wrong. You could smell it from here to Texas. As for Thurlow, don't let him fool you. He looks like God's gift to humanity, but he's still a banker. He made an investment. He wasn't satisfied with the interest he was getting." Temple crossed his bony shanks. "Whitworth was sponsored by the judge. Emerson was supposed to be the entering wedge in our campaign to oust the Churlak faction, but it wasn't doing much in the way of prying the lid off. You couldn't blame Marvin for wanting to know why."

"I see." Jessie smiled pleasantly. "But if you're not involved, why is a police detective watching your place?"

Temple was startled. "Watching my place?"

"He's standing across the street." Jessie leaned forward. "Do you think perhaps Judge Nichol put the police up to it?"

Temple came out of his chair. "Nichol?"

"The police are afraid of him. He's important. They don't want to embarrass him." Jessie leaned even farther forward, her tone confidential. "Not even when I showed them they've got a better case against his own daughter than they have against Mrs. Whitworth."

Temple's voice turned sharp. "You showed them that?"

69

Jessie nodded. "Don't tell me you disapprove. It's in your favor as well. Emerson's out of the running. Means more of the brunette's time for you."

"Miss Starbuck, excuse me for being blunt, but . . . Cyrene Yarbrough is anybody's woman and everybody's woman." He turned to Ki, his stare piercing, direct. "From what I hear she was yours last night."

Ki grinned noncommittally.

Jessie wondered where Temple had heard it. She thought it might have been from Chief Weims, though the detective across the street seemed to indicate that Temple and the chief weren't exactly exchanging confidences. She wondered if Temple were really as callous about Cyrene as he sounded.

So she pried. "Did the brunette take you for much?"

Temple sat back down, rigid. "Don't be absurd."

"She took Emerson."

"How do you know?"

"Well, somebody took him," Jessie insisted. "Funny you men on the council weren't able to find that out for yourselves. All you had to do was what Harold Whitworth did—ask. Emerson being broke suggest anything to you?"

"Should it?"

Jessie planted her second charge of dynamite for the day. "It would be interesting to check into his past, Mr. Temple, and find out where all the money went."

Temple's mouth tightened. "That's what you intend to do?"

"I might as well," Jessie said, moving toward the doorway. "I've got a lot of time to kill while they're looking for Millicent Whitworth."

She departed with Ki. Outside, they nodded politely to Detective Brody across the street and went on to a nearby restaurant, where they stopped for lunch. Afterward they proceeded to the Lincoln State Bank & Trust, a prosperous-looking institution. The customers, too, looked prosperous, though not all of them looked happy. Unlike Ike Temple, the guiding spirit of all this pleasant bustle was readily accessible. In fact Thurlow Dobbs was in plain sight, moving amiably about the main banking room, a rotund cherub.

"How do you do, Miss Starbuck!" His voice was a genial thunderclap, his hand as pink and soft as a baby's bottom. He gestured toward the open door of an office. "Step inside, won't you?" Crossing the moderately crowded rotunda with them, he kept up a running fore of "Hello John"s and "How are you, Mary"s.

Everybody appeared to be fine. Jessie thought that if she were asked by Dobbs, she would be fine, too. In the office, with the door closed, she let out her breath carefully, a little at a time.

"Do you do that all day?"

"And every day," Dobbs said, and mopped sweat from his face. "It's wearing, but it's what makes Lincoln State successful." He sank into an enormous swivel chair. The desk was outsize, too, and cluttered with trifles that said that here was no cold fish of a banker. "Darned unfortunate about Emerson. Unfortunate not only for the Reform Council, but for his wife and daughter."

"You don't believe Mrs. Emerson shot him?"

"Do you?"

"I don't know." Jessie hesitated. "Put it this way: If Emerson shot Whitworth, then I'll give you Mrs. Whitworth as a fifty-fifty choice as the killer of Emerson."

"Fifty-fifty?" Dobbs thought that over for a minute. "Who's the other one?"

"Alderman Churlak and Chief Weims are two. The alderman isn't exactly crying over the emptiness of the district attorney's office," Jessie said. Then she added carefully, "How do you feel about Judge Nichol?"

Dobbs gave a start. "You're not suggesting—"

"He knew what Whitworth was doing. So did Ike Temple. So did you."

"But you don't think—"

"I think Whitworth was killed as a lead-up to killing Emerson. Don't ask me why I think that, just chalk it up to feminine intuition if you have to. It's more of a hope—the only answer I can get if I want to believe Millicent Whitworth didn't shoot Emerson."

The chair creaked under Dobbs's weight. He wasn't jovial any longer. "You mention this to anyone else?"

Jessie nodded. "As my daddy taught me, when you don't know what you're doing, you light a fire under everybody and sort of hope something boils to the surface."

"You've lit a fire under me."

"Well, perhaps. Not with as much hope, though. You're about the only one who doesn't seem to have a reason for hating Emerson." Through lidded eyes she watched the broad moon face opposite her. "The twenty-five thousand you invested in his election would be a drop in the bucket to you. All there is left, I suppose, is jealousy."

"Jealousy? Oh, you must be referring to the brunette."

Jessie nodded. "Like her?"

"Not that much."

"Who is she?"

Dobbs looked uncomfortable. "She trades with us. As far as I know, she's just a lady with plenty of money and a yen for men. I don't mean to imply she's promiscuous," he added hastily, "not in the strictest physical sense." He got up, went to the door, looked out, and shut it again. "Is she on your list, too?"

"For only one reason," Jessie answered, thinking there were actually two—the second being her spending the night with Ki. That might have been arranged so he'd be out of circulation while somebody ganged up on Mrs. Whitworth. Keeping that idea to herself, Jessie said, "You mentioned that she had plenty of money, Mr. Dobbs. I thought maybe it might have come to her fairly recently." She stood up. "Among other things I'm looking for the money that Emerson had and lost. He had around a hundred thousand when he moved his account from here to Illinois National. You must have a record of the transactions before that. I'd like to look at them."

Dobbs hesitated. "Can do," he said finally. "Anyone else you're interested in?"

"Sure. Churlak, Weims, Nichol, Temple—it wouldn't hurt to know about the finances of all of them. And which ones have safety deposit boxes."

"That'll take a little time, I'm afraid."

"I'm in no hurry."

The fat banker sighed. "And all this is leading up to what?"

"It depends on where we start. Me, I think it starts back before Whitworth joined your council. Somewhere, possibly in Emerson's past. You might prepare me a little digest of that, too, while you're at it." She started for the lobby door, falling in behind. "Thank you for everything."

Dobbs's chuckle was a delighted rumble. "You left out my account. I'm hurt."

"Very well, you can put that in, too," Jessie said.

She and Ki went out through the busy rotunda and stepped into the bright afternoon sunshine. Heading back to their hotel, they came to the tall *News-Dispatch* building. Jessie paused thoughtfully by its entrance.

"Ki," she said after a moment, "I'd like you to go in and see the city editor, or whoever's in charge of the story about the killings. Tell him that you're spokesman for Starbuck Purveyors, and you're offering a twenty-thousand-dollar reward for information as to the whereabouts of Millicent. Whoop it up good, make it sound important."

"It is, isn't it?"

"Well, yes, although I've got a sinking feeling we won't be getting any takers. Anyway, while you're doing that, I'll go over to the telegraph office and wire the Circle Star for any information on this passel of hombres we've run into. I'll meet you back at the Metropole."

Leaving Ki, Jessie continued on through the sidewalk swirl of traffic. Halfway along the next block, two men she had never seen before ranged themselves alongside of her—bulky men who might have been cops, but weren't. One was short and very wide; his florid face seemed to consist mostly of nose. The other had a natty brown mustache emphasizing his younger, sleeker body.

"Going our way, lady?"

Fingers like iron bruised the bones of her forearms. The man on her right had his hat off, his free hand inside the hat. Jessie didn't think the hand would be empty. She had the wild impulse to scream; then she remembered her and Ki's own ambush of Gregory Boothroyd under almost the same circumstances.

"Listen," she said earnestly. "Garibaldi isn't going to like this."

The hands on her arms, the bulk of their bodies, urged her toward the line of tethered horses and wagons at the curb. "You got us wrong, lady. We just heard you were a drinkin' dame, so we're gonna show you where you can wet your whistle."

Jessie tried to wrench her arms free, couldn't, pushed herself backward and launched a terrific kick at the nearest ankle. She missed. Something that could have been a sledgehammer hit her in the throat. Swift, blinding agony engulfed her; then, mercifully, darkness . . .

She was in a wagon. The sway of the box, the creak of wheels told her this; by the smell of rotted produce, she could tell it was a grocery wagon. Presently, through waves of sickening pain, she isolated facts: She was on the floor of the wagon bed; she was bound hand and foot, and there was a blindfold over her eyes, a gag over her mouth. She wondered why they had bothered to do this. She was wracked by a fit of retching, made more horrible by the seal on her mouth.

She passed out again.

★

Chapter 6

Wind bathed her face, wind with the smell of water and the sharp pungency of conifers. She was no longer in the wagon. She was on a cot, a smelly cot, with a sheet over her. Regaining consciousness slowly, woozily, she became aware before opening her eyes or mouth that their covering had been removed; so had most of her clothes, down to her lacy chemise.

Above her a voice said, "Maybe we should've just put a slug in her."

"And get pinched for shooting outa season?" There was a raucous laugh. "Besides, Leo, Marie wouldn't have stood for it. Seems nuts to me to've brung a dame in on this."

"We got one already, whether we like it or not. We need a woman to guard a woman, Pocker, 'specially considerin' this's Marie's cabin. I don't want us to do nothin' while it's still daylight, and we might get spotted." The gruff-voiced man named Leo leaned closer. "Think she can hear us?"

"I dunno." Pocker laughed again. "Can you hear us, lady? We promised you a drink, remember? Well, you're gonna get it—a whole lake full."

Quite suddenly Jessie knew where she was. She knew where Millicent Whitworth was, too. She wondered if she would actually see the widow, there at the bottom of Lake Michigan. Figuring she couldn't help herself playing possum any longer, she opened her eyes and clutched the sheet up around her neck. "Who are you?" she demanded.

Leo, the younger man, replied. "Police. Where's your bodyguard?"

"I don't know," she answered dully. "Let me get dressed."

The heavyset Pocker gestured at her clothes dumped on a chair. "Sure. Go put 'em on."

"If you'll leave the room."

He looked at the two open windows. "I bet you'd like us to. If you wanna get dressed, go get 'em, or I'll drag you outta bed like you are." He grabbed one corner of the sheet and giggled in a way that chilled her.

The door to the bedroom suddenly opened, and a woman in a blue print dress entered, frowning. She was on either side of thirty, overpainted, full-blown, slow-moving. Men who liked elaborately curved women would have considered her attractive. To Jessie she looked big and tough and hard.

"Give her a chance," the woman said sharply.

Pocker stepped back. Jessie sat up, keeping the sheet up across the bodice of her low-cut chemise, and slipped out of the far side of the bed, her back to the men. The chair was next to the open door. The woman, Marie, stepped aside so she could reach her clothing. Jessie rummaged through the pile, searching for her chatelaine purse. It wasn't there; either she had lost it or her captors had taken it away, having discovered the derringer in it, along with the pistol in her jacket. She was unarmed, virtually defenseless. In a frantic attempt to escape, she leapt for the main room—the only other room in the cabin—praying the front door was unlocked.

Hands caught her before she crossed the threshold. She started to scream, but a thick, sweaty palm clamped over her mouth and cut off the sound before it passed her throat. Her left wrist was caught in a powerful grip; her arm was twisted behind her back and pushed up between her shoulder blades. Her body jerked, the sheet dropped, and the hand clamped on her mouth choked back another cry of pain. As she writhed, she heard a giggle in her ear, and that told her that it was Pocker, the wide man, who was inflicting the torture. She sagged. He held her up against him and exerted a little more pressure on her arm.

"Let her go," Leo said quietly.

She almost collapsed when Pocker released her. She stumbled away from him, rubbing her burning arm.

Pocker giggled. "I wasn't gonna break her arm," he explained to Leo. "Just teach her not to try funny business."

"I'll do the teaching," Leo said. He was lounging against the bedroom bureau, rolling a cigarette. Lighting it, he blew smoke at her. "You want to get dressed, Miz Starbuck? Marie will stay with you. You try anything like this again, I'll take off your clothes and beat the skin off you with my belt."

He said it without emotion, and his pale eyes were expressionless, but she knew that he meant it. And she knew that this quiet, muscular man was much more deadly than the inanely giggling thug.

Wearily she returned to the bed; the arm Pocker had twisted continued to throb, but that was only physical pain. The agony of terror inside her was much harder to bear.

Closing the door, Marie sat on the bed, crossed her

knees, and watched Jessie. "Pocker always had an eye for a pretty figure," she said.

Jessie glanced out the nearest window, looking out across the yard to an outhouse, a small but powerful two-holer concealed by tall brush. "I have to go," she said.

"Go? Go where?"

"*Go!* You know."

Marie shrugged, said, "C'mon," and went out of the bedroom with Jessie.

Pocker snarled, "So what?" when Marie told the men where she was taking Jessie—and why. "She ain't going nowhere, for no reason."

Leo looked out the main-room window at the outhouse, then back to Pocket. "Let her do what she wants." It was obvious that he was anxious to keep his captive appeased on small matters, to make her feel as much at ease as possible so that he would not have a hysterical woman on his hands until dark.

Maria marched Jessie out the front door and along a dirt path to the outhouse. Jessie went inside. Marie closed the door and, by the sound of it, leaned against the planks, grumbling to herself.

Jessie did not have to go, except to go as far from here as possible as soon as possible. She had no specific plan in mind, but had figured that before she risked knocking Marie unconscious in the bedroom, she should see if the outhouse offered a better chance of escape. Well, perhaps she was in a bit of luck—there was a screened window for ventilation high on the rear wall, square and small, but she thought she might be able to squeeze through it.

That is, if she could get rid of Marie first.

Jessie started grunting and groaning.

"What's the matter in there?" Marie demanded.

"I've got the runs," Jessie moaned, playing for time.

The outhouse was old, and the stench that had built up over time was ferocious, foul enough to make Jessie's eyes water. She sat on the edge of the two-hole seat, her mind going over the details of what she would do. She would act sick, lure Marie inside, then chop her in the neck the way Ki had trained her. Odds were she would fail—that Marie would not be completely knocked out or that she would manage to cry out or that the men in the cabin would hear or see her fall. But whatever the chances of failure, she had no alternative.

Marie cursed. "You gonna shit in there all day?"

"I told you, I . . . I'm ill."

"I'll die if I don't get away from this stink," Marie complained. "I'll be back in a moment, and you'd better be through!"

Incredulously, Jessie heard the woman start back along the path to the cabin. Instantly she climbed on the seat under the high, small window. She heard Pocker swearing loudly, asking Marie what was the fuckin' idea.

"She's got the runs," Marie replied. "Besides, we got her clothes. That kind of girl wouldn't go running around half-naked."

"Get back out there!"

"Okay, okay, only first let me get my tobacco chaw."

Jessie pushed out the screen, hoisted herself to the windowsill, and went through headfirst. Momentarily her hips stopped her. The hook at the bottom of the screen raked her body as she squirmed through; then the swinging screen smacked her feet, but in her frenzy, minor pain was meaningless. She fell to the ground behind the outhouse. Breathlessly she sat there, but only for a moment. The scraping of the outhouse door roused her. As she leapt to her feet, she heard Marie yell, "Where are you? You fall in?"

Then Jessie was running on bare feet over the hard, stubbled ground.

The woods were a hundred feet from the outhouse. There was not much to them—a narrow strip of scrub oak and birch and brush, ending a quarter of a mile away at a wagon road curving along two sides of the woods, with open meadows on the right. Behind her somebody shouted. She glanced back. Pocker was rounding the corner of the cabin.

"I'll shoot!"

She had almost reached the trees. Her lungs burned, her legs wobbled, but desperation drove her on. She turned her head; Pocker was racing after her, cutting the distance between them, and Leo was behind him. A gunshot blasted behind her. She ducked reflexively, feeling a sting of slivers from bark off a tree immediately to her right. Then she dove into the woods at the footpath that ran through to the wagon road. She hesitated, knowing that if she stuck to the path, they would easily catch her. On her left, also toward the road, where it curved, the woods were open, and there, too, she'd be seen in a matter of moments. There was only one way left—the solid mass of blackberry bushes on her right.

She plunged. Sharp thorns tore at her chemise, at her flesh. Throwing her hands in front of her face, she pushed on. Her bare toes struck something, a stone, a root, and she stumbled, but it was from sheer exhaustion that she fell. There was no strength left in her to rise, and that was what saved her. She lay on a comparatively bare spot of ground, completely surrounded by the bushes, and the pursuit went past her.

Tiny darts of fire pitted her legs and arms and the backs of her hands where the thorns had ripped. But she had to move on, and the only way was through the bushes. Bare-legged and bare-armed and wearing only that skimpy chemise, it was madness to try. But it was death not to.

She started to rise, and suddenly the voices of the two men were back. They stopped very close to her. She dug her teeth into her bare forearm to keep back the moans of pain and panic.

"Damn Marie!" Leo was saying. "I ought to break her neck for letting that Starbuck gal get away."

"Yeah, well, where'd she go?"

"Maybe through these bushes."

Jessie hardly breathed.

"She'd be ripped to shreds," Pocker said.

"See this bush crushed like somebody went through it?"

Jessie flexed her muscles to leap up and plunge on.

"What's on the other side?" Pocker asked.

"Fields. Wide fields it'll take her maybe ten minutes to get across. And she can't go fast enough through these bushes. Right near the cabin there's a little hill where we can spot her."

"Any houses nearby?"

"Not near the fields." Leo swore. "C'mon, we're wasting time. You take the road. I'll take the fields."

Jessie did not hear them depart, but again it was silent. They'd return, though, soon as they figured she had to be hiding in this strip of the woods. She forced herself to wait several long minutes, then slowly stood erect. Leo's range of vision from the knoll would cover the fields, she reckoned; she could not escape that way. She thought for a second of doubling back to the cabin, but in all likelihood Marie would be there, smarting for revenge. That left the nearby road—and Pocker, if Pocker chanced to be where he could spot her. But that was the risk she'd have to take.

Keeping her hands in front of her face, Jessie made her way out of the blackberry bushes. The tormenting thorns were easier to bear now that escape was so close. She ducked across the path and ran parallel with it. She thought she heard whinnying, the rumble of wagon wheels. A patch of cloudless sky ahead grew larger. And then she was on the top of a ten-foot embankment, with the narrow, rutted, hardpan road below.

With the hem of her chemise she wiped up the blood on her legs and arms and face. She leaned forward, searching the road. Both sides of it were visible up to the sharp curve two hundred feet to her left, and there was no man or woman in sight. Only the embankment itself afforded a hiding place, and she could reach the road as quickly as anybody else on the embankment. She climbed down.

A farm wagon was rolling from the east, driven by a team of draft horses. On the wagon seat was an elderly couple, the wispy-bearded man wearing bib overalls, the gray-haired woman beside him dressed in a flowery Mother Hubbard. Jessie found level ground under her bare feet and ran out into the middle of the road. "Stop!" She was aware of the fantastic picture she made, bare-footed and skimpily clad and somewhat bloody; but that would be all the more reason for the couple to stop for her.

The farmer pulled on the reins, whoa-ing the team, and the wagon stopped some fifty feet from where she stood. Breathlessly she hastened toward it—only to spot another wagon approaching rapidly from behind, a closed-bed grocery wagon driven by Marie, who was whipping her galloping horses in an attempt to overtake Jessie. Pocker was already jumping to the ground, lunging toward her. Jessie pivoted, angling away to avoid Pocker and springing for the embankment. His powerful fingers closed over her arm.

Clawing at his face, Jessie screamed for help. She glimpsed the farm couple scrambling down from their wagon, and she subsided a little. Certainly in front of witnesses she had no reason to fear recapture. Pocker smiled tightly. His fist moved only a few inches from her jaw. Jessie didn't feel herself fall, but all of a sudden she was lying on the road and there was a strange lack of control over her muscles. She could see as through a gray veil, and she could hear as from a distance, but she couldn't move.

Her shoulders were being raised from the ground. She tried to stand; one arm actually rose a few inches, then flapped limply. Vaguely she was aware of the couple standing about her.

"You shouldn't have hit her like that," the farmer was saying.

Whoever held her shoulders was giggling, and she knew that it was Pocker. He said, "Look at her. Dead drunk. Runnin' around with practically nothin' on. I gotta get her home."

The farmer's wife said indignantly, "Her mouth is bleeding. You hurt her."

"Naw," Pocker said. "I wouldn't hurt my own wife."

He had Jessie under the armpits and was dragging her. Her bare heels burned as they scraped over the road. There was blood in her mouth and her jaw was numb and she could only moan. This was a nightmare in which she was aware of a terrible thing happening to her, but could not make herself wake up.

"Serves you right for marrying that tramp," a woman scolded. The voice was familiar, and sluggishly Jessie decided that it belonged to Marie. "I told you from the first she was no good."

"Well, I married her and I'm responsible for her," Pocker said. "Help me get her into the wagon."

Hands grasped Jessie's bare ankles. She felt herself being lifted off the ground, and then something solid was under her back. No! In the grocery wagon again, she'd be completely in their power. She had to find her voice, her strength.

"You're okay, baby," Pocker told her kindly. "I'm taking you home to bed."

Her voice burst out of her. "Save me! He— He—!"

A brutal hand clamped over her mouth; a knee dug into her chest. She heard the door at the back of the wagon close. She was inside the wagon, on the floor of the bed, and the farm couple outside couldn't see what he was doing to her, or wouldn't interfere if they did.

"Looks like she's getting the d.t.'s," Marie was explaining to the couple. "I don't care what her husband says, I'd have her committed."

Then the wagon was moving, taking her away from the people who could have saved her. The pressure of Pocker's knee on her chest became an unendurable weight as he leaned foward, giggling, staring at her with hungry little eyes. Despite her pain, her fear, Jessie made herself send him a smoldering smile.

Pocker eased up, grinning like a small boy offered candy.

"You—you're so strong," Jessie gasped, sucking air into her lungs. "Too strong for me." She placed a hand on his shoulder. "I like big, strong men."

He leaned over her, very still. In their fatty sockets his eyes shifted to the front of the enclosed bed, where under the front overhang of the roof, Marie sat with her back to them, hurrahing the team into a gallop. Suddenly Pocker slashed his arm upward, knocking Jessie's hand off his shoulder.

"A wise floozy," he said with a sneer. "What're you after—my gun?"

His blow had numbed her forearm. She held it tightly and shivered as though in defeat and shame. Damn right she was after his gun, or the knife he had sheathed on his belt—any weapon she could grab onto. Which meant she had to lure Pocker closer, off guard. "You're afraid of Leo," she taunted.

"Hell I am!"

"If you weren't afraid, we could make a deal," Jessie purred. "I don't want to die. I want to live—and I'll do anything, *anything*, if you'll let me live."

"Anything . . . ?"

She lay swaying as the wagon rumbled along, hugging herself, smiling provocatively up at Pocker leering over her. "You promise you'll let me go?"

"Sure, sure, it's a deal." Pocker broadened his grin, as if telling himself that fear had driven her into hysteria and that he had nothing to lose and maybe a lot to gain by humoring her. "O' course, I gotta check out your part o' the deal first." He hooked a finger in the low-cut nape of her filmy chemise, ogling her exposed breasts.

That was when Jessie struck. She reached down between them with her right hand and grabbed hold of his scrotum, squeezing and twisting with all her might. While Pocker was momentarily distracted, with her left hand Jessie unsheathed his knife and pushed the blade up into his heart. The point struck bone, slid by; the blade went in up to the handle.

Pocker uttered a horrible gurgling sound. His hand moved toward her throat, then fell away. All of him was rolling away from her. For an instant bulging eyes in which the pupils seemed to have vanished stared at her, and she saw blood spurt past the knife and spray her chemise. Then his shoulders struck the floor, and he came to rest beside her, and she heard Marie's voice.

"Pocker?" She had heard that dying gurgle but evidently did not understand what it was. "Hey, Pocker?" She turned on the seat, stared at Jessie. "Je-sus!"

Jessie snatched up Pocker's gun. "Stop the wagon!"

"You got Pocker's gun!" Marie blurted, too panic-stricken to obey Jessie's order. She did a weird little dance, standing and lurching a step to her right and a step backward, then leaping, squalling, off the side of the wagon. Her cry ended abruptly as she hit the hardpan surface of the road.

The team, as if catching the scent of fear, plunged faster ahead. Bracing herself against the violently rocking wagon, Jessie lurched toward the seat Marie had just vacated. She managed a grabbing catch of the reins, which had almost slid off the front dashboard and down between the team, but made no attempt to slow the horses. Directly ahead lay the cabin; behind, she could see Marie stumbling off into the woods, bawling for Leo. Every second counted, so she let the horses run the remaining distance to the cabin before hauling in the reins, and applying the foot brake with as much pressure as she could muster.

Halting, she sprang down and sprinted into the cabin, where she grabbed her clothes and her bag, which she found in the bedroom wardrobe after a quick, frantic search. She found her derringer still tucked in the bag, but couldn't readily locate her custom pistol and didn't have the time for a thorough hunt. She took what she had and rushed back out to the wagon.

Tossing her belongings into the back, she whipped the team into a fast gallop and tore out of the yard. Behind her she could hear approaching shouts and a rattle of gunfire, but crouching on the seat up front, protected by the wagon's enclosed box, she couldn't tell if any of the hastily fired bullets even came close. Another moment and she was rounding a curve in the road, passing from sight of the cabin and heading, she hoped, toward Chicago.

Ah, but where in Chicago could she go? Back to the hotel wasn't safe; most likely it was being watched, and even if it weren't her showing up the way she looked would certainly bring attention. The Whitworth home?

No, that might require breaking into, and it most certainly was under surveillance. Phillip Bolanger was the only other person she could turn to right now ... assuming she could find, much less remember, his address.

★
Chapter 7

Hours later, well into the night, Jessie finally located Phillip Bolanger's modest home. Despite her exhaustion, pain, and trepidation, she couldn't help admiring the spray of stars above Chicago and the glow of moon toying with the city shadows. It was sufficiently brilliant to bathe the streets and the silent, dark-windowed bungalow. Evidently Bolanger was asleep.

Well, not for long.

Although there had been no further incidents since her escape from Marie's cabin, Jessie had not risked stopping once, not even to get dressed. Nor did she take any chances now, hurriedly tethering the wagon team to a nearby post and hastening barefooted, still clad in only her chemise, up the walk to the front stoop of Bolanger's house. She banged on the door with her fists, loudly calling his name.

A commotion arose from within, as though someone had fallen out of bed. Then came a hurried padding of feet, and the door opened. Bolanger stood peering out, bleary-eyed, mouth agape, wearing only his trousers. "Jessie! Gawd, we've been worried sick, been looking all over for you!"

Swiftly Jessie brushed past him and closed the door behind her. "You didn't quite look everywhere," she sighed, collapsing into a soft chair—and then stiffening upright, groaning involuntarily from the pain of her bruises and lacerations.

Bolanger lit a glass standing lamp and hunkered beside her, shaking his head. "Good grief, you look like you done fell in a briar patch and then rolled in garbage."

"Close. Thorns and a grocery wagon bed, to be exact."

Flustered and embarrassed, Bolanger acted as though he weren't sure whether he should be looking or not. Jessie's thin chemise was torn and filthy, only loosely containing her voluptuous breasts. "You can't stay thisaway," he said and tentatively touched her back. "Bend forward a tad, if you can."

She leaned over, biting her lip, feeling him gently peel away the ripped fabric of her chemise that was stuck to her thorn-slashed flesh.

"Don't look too deep. More dirty'n anything," he said, still frowning with concern. "My guess is, with a bath and a bandagin' and a good smear of ointment, your cuts oughta heal up right fine."

She tried to make light of it. "Nary a scar, Doctor?"

"Probably not, if we treat it right soon. I'm no doc, though."

"I need a bath in any case. Is there a chance . . . ?"

"Why, sure. Stay put." He made two trips out of the room, one for wood with which to stoke the cast-iron Dutch oven, and the other for water to fill the washtub he placed on the stove's burners. While the water was heating, he hauled out a heavy tin bathtub and placed it near the stove.

"This isn't the height of modesty," he said, beginning to redden around the ears. "But while you're washing, I'll go fetch the doc."

"No, I don't want a doctor, thank you," Jessie replied, managing to keep a serious expression. She trailed him into the small bedroom, saying, "I don't want anyone to know I'm here."

"Not even Ki?"

"Not yet, not until I know I can show myself safely."

"Well, you can feel safe showin' yourself here. I mean, er ..." He trailed off with a thick gulp and began ransacking a tall wardrobe. "Now, I know I've got a clean towel in here somewheres. What happened?"

In a quick, brief summary, Jessie recounted the events.

Bolanger was outraged. "Those stinkin' dogs! We'll have to inform the police, naturally, and get them out huntin'. I'm not sure how much good it'll do; I doubt Chief Weims could find his hat in a sealed room." He handed Jessie a towel. "Here, this's the biggest I got."

The towel was the size of a child's blanket. Jessie refolded it and laid it on a table next to the stove. "If you want to go do something, go take the wagon around back somewhere out of sight, and bring in my clothes."

"Will do." Bolanger brooded for a moment, then stepped closer, searching her eyes. "Jessie, you'd best leave Chicago as soon as you can."

"Leave? I don't plan on leaving, but on staying."

"I want you to stay, too, of course, but you must leave, for your own sake. This is a local power struggle, and I won't have you dying in a fight that isn't your own."

"This *is* my fight, Phil. More than you know."

"You've already risked your life as much as any man would. More!" He gripped her tenderly by the shoulders. "Garibaldi and all these other crooks won't stop at nothing. They've already proved they won't stop at brutalizing and killing a woman."

Bolanger heard her sigh in agreement, as she pressed her cheek against his chest. It seemed so natural for her to melt in his arms, as natural as lowering his face to kiss her, the pressure of her body like an eager promise. Shaken and chagrined, Bolanger released her, taking a step backward. "F-forgive me, Jessie, I didn't mean to be forward."

Jessie looked as though she weren't paying the slightest attention to his apology. She placed the open palm of one hand flat against his cheek. "You could use a shave," she said, stroking upward against the stubble. "When I rub down, it's smooth, and when I rub up, you're all whiskers."

Bolanger shivered, speechless from her caress, staring at her affectionate smile. There were rents in her chemise, and one side was almost torn away. Bloodstains and scratches marred her smooth, tanned face and delicate hands, and her long hair, tangled and hatless, gleamed like fireweed honey where the glowing fire reflected against it. She was a lovely thing, and Bolanger battled hard to retain his control.

"The, ah, water is warm," he finally managed, blushing to his hairline. "We ... I mean, you can have a nice bath now."

Hastily he poured the steaming water into the plunge tub, tossed in a bar of soap, and fled for the front door. "Soak as long as you like."

"I will," she replied lightly, shedding her chemise. She washed carefully, thoroughly, wanting to be squeaky clean in case anything developed—which, considering Bolanger's flustered behavior, was not entirely impossible.

She was not a promiscuous wanton, the victim of an insatiable sex drive. It was simply that she was not a prude or a hypocrite; she was pure woman, proud of her femininity, and she relished the sensation of being attractive to men she found desirable. And Lord, was

Phillip Bolanger desirable! She had thought so ever since their first meeting, and thinking of him now caused her taut breasts to tingle. The easy grace of his motions, the strong muscles flexing along his thighs and chest, the hard bas-relief of his loins in his pants . . .

Whoops! Jessie straightened in the tub, chastising herself. It was one thing to admire him, or even to desire him; it was quite another to get herself worked into a frazzle.

She stepped out of the tub, and was reaching for the towel when she heard the back door open in the bedroom. "Is that you, Phil?"

"Yeah. I got your clothes."

"Well, don't peek. I'm having trouble with this towel of yours." She stepped away from the tub, the towel perversely slipping and unraveling, no matter how she tried to hold it closed. She could glimpse him in the dim bedroom, putting her clothes on a chair. She struggled to raise the hem of the towel over her breasts, but at the cost of one edge of the towel behind her parting like an errant stage curtain and fully, if briefly, exposing her firm buttocks and lithely tapering thighs.

Bolanger dropped her boots.

Jessie retreated, scampering. "I said not to peek!"

"I didn't see a thing, Jessie. Honest!" There was a pause; then Bolanger asked, "Was there something you wanted?"

"Well, you told me my cuts need ointment and bandages, and I can't very well reach all the way around my back and do it, can I?"

"Oh." There was another pause, longer and somehow more profound. Then, nervously: "I, eh, I'll do it. You go get arranged on my bed, and I'll get the stuff with my back turned."

He turned his back and began rummaging in his bureau drawers. Jessie entered the bedroom and stretched out on her stomach on the iron-framed single bed, very carefully making sure the towel was draped properly over her from the waist down.

Bolanger turned, clearing his throat a lot, and put a roll of gauze bandages, scissors, and a tin of ointment on the bedside table. He sat down, balancing on the edge of the bed with all the caution of a man expecting the mattress to explode.

"Just consider me one of the Starbuck Purveyor cows," Jessie said, hoping to relax him, her face buried in the covers. "I'll moo, if it'll help."

With a tight chuckle, Bolanger opened the tin and began to spread the ointment hesitantly along her wounds. It burned like a branding iron.

"My God, Phil, what is that stuff? Acid?"

"Arnicated carbolic salve," he answered, pausing to quote the label: " 'The best in the world for burns, flesh injuries, boils, eczema, chilblains, piles, ulcers, and fever sores.' " He started smoothing it on again, assuring her, "My dad swore by it for his salt rheum and ringworm. Don't worry. It'll smart for just a minute, and then it'll just feel nice 'n' warm."

Jessie lay still, skeptically waiting for the salve to stop burning and start warming. Amazingly it did, the warmth penetrating while Bolanger continued rubbing gingerly with his fingers. He leaned over her back, so close that she could feel his breath against her flesh and smell the fragrance of his masculine body ... and gradually, she sensed budding tendrils of pleasure beginning to curl deep down in her belly and loins and gently clenching buttocks.

Bolanger continued to touch her softly. Massaging, kneading, his hands easing from high along her sides, down her spine to the dimple of flesh just above the crevice of her tensing buttocks. His fingers explored very slowly, almost fearfully, and she could hear his breath deepening, his pulse quickening. And she could feel her own lungs sucking in air, her blood racing with a fire that flamed through her flesh and goaded her to reckless abandon.

She turned over. A slight twinge of self-consciousness stole through her as she sat up, facing him, and saw his eyes roaming heatedly over her naked, thrusting breasts. "You're undressing me naked with your eyes," she teased in a throbbing voice.

His own voice was husky. "Sorry, Jessie, that's twice now that I've . . . I don't know what's come over me."

"There's nothing to be sorry about." Intimacy crept into her tone, and she touched his arm. "Only to be happy about," she continued in a silky purr, her other hand pulling the towel aside. "You want me. After all, I'm a woman and you're a man . . ."

His tongue licked his lips to moisten them, as he stared, quivering, at her delicately molded thighs and golden-fleeced loins. Desire stirred within him, despite his best intentions.

"N-no, Jessie, you're not mine to take. You're my boss!"

"Then I'll direct you," she murmured tauntingly, reaching down to unbuckle his belt. "And you follow my lead, all right?"

And Bolanger found himself moving, his body responding of its own volition. His fingers fumbled with the buttons, his hips trembling as he rose to slide his pants down, his flesh aching as Jessie ran her hands around his chest and thighs while helping him rid himself of his pants. Then he was as naked as she, tanned and muscular and admirably masculine.

Bolanger joined her on the bed, his mouth coming down on hers. He kissed her and she kissed back, and fire was in their lips. Awkward with passion, he tried to push her flat and enter her from above, but the pressure against her wounds was too painful for her to accept. "Phil," she whispered. "My back."

He reared as if scalded. "Jessie, we can't—"

"We can." She drew away slightly, just enough so she could turn and crouch on her knees and elbows with her buttocks thrusting up, in what many called the cow-hitch position. "Moo," she said.

Bolanger was eagerly game to try playing the bull. He slid behind her on his knees and took her gently, his hands gliding along her sides and up around to fondle her breasts. He moved deep within her, and Jessie felt him clearly, with a joy that surged through her. It was this elation that made her anchor her feet against the bed, raising her hips to press up and back to match his passionate thrusts. The world burst in a rainbow of colors, but in reality there was no world for Jessie just then—there was only his throbbing, this pulsing rhythm inside her gripping belly. Together they worked in frenzied ecstasy, until at last they reached sweet release, and he spilled his passion deep inside her while she squeezed around him, shuddering.

Bolanger sprawled beside her on the cramped bed, his erection fading, his breathing trembling in her ear. But greater indeed was the fulfillment inside Jessie, the effervescent sensation of contentment and satiation. Stirring, she eased from the bed, reaching back with one hand to retrieve the blanket.

"No," Bolanger said, smiling up at her. "No blanket."

"But Phil," she teased, standing naked beside the bed, "what about your modesty that you were so worried about?"

He laughed. "Too late for that, li'l heifer."

She sashayed to the doorway and stood there in the warmth from the stove, feeling no embarrassment at all. She felt pleased and natural, basking in his adoring gaze, admiring in return his openly displayed, handsome body.

He rose on an elbow. "You've got me going in circles, y'know."

"About what?"

"You. Us. This."

Smiling, she parried. "You mean, about having sex?"

"Yeah, in a way. I guess I'll never figure women out. A man, now, is pretty straightforward. I've never been much for the notion that there's just one woman in the world for a man, but all the other women I've met up with before don't seem to agree."

"Then it's simple, Phil. You've merely met up with a woman as straightforward as you, who agrees with you." She crossed to the bed and knelt beside him, and as he put out his hand to caress one of her distended nipples, she whispered, "Make it as good as the last time."

Bolanger ran his hand over the mounds of her breasts and down across her smooth belly to the soft, pulsing warmth below. Jessie moaned, her flesh coming alive to his caresses, and her voice sighed in his ear, urging him to quench the fires kindling in her loins.

He kissed her lips, her cheeks, the tender hollow of her neck. Slipping lower, he darted his tongue across her hardened nipples, then moved it wetly along her abdomen, feeling the satiny skin ripple under his tauntings. Then, still lower, his lips probed and explored as she cried out in ecstatic pleasure. She rolled from side to side while he licked at her inner lips; she whimpered deliriously as her throbbing arousal increased, her fingers entangled in his hair.

The splayed thighs beneath his mouth arched and swiveled. Bolanger gave them room. Jessie again stretched out alongside him, but now facing the foot of the bed, her legs still spread wide on either side of his bobbing head. Bolanger could feel her hands move from his hair and down along his body, clutching his buttocks, pulling him toward her face. Her tongue began teasing him, dancing like a waterbug on the crown of his erection. Bolanger pressed her loins harder against his sucking mouth, and a deep animal sound escaped from his nibbling lips.

Below, between his own widely stretched legs, Jessie dipped farther, licking along his rigid shaft and then plunging her mouth voraciously over it, swallowing it in a soft, clinging pressure. Bolanger felt his hips writhing, stirring, swaying, his entire body seeming to swim in a vast sea of tense sensation.

Jessie's seemingly disembodied lips, her mouth, her throat were eating him, trying to draw the whole of him into her yearning flesh. Bolanger could distinguish no external detail of touch. Doubtless her teeth were there, nipping gently; her tongue was there, licking and twining; her lips were there, pressing and sucking ... but no detail was clear, only the combining vacuum of suction drawing all of his vital juices down to his groin.

And in response to her own urgent yearnings, Jessie was pressing her naked body full-length against him, undulating back and forth, around and up, so that the potent force of his tongue was being drawn deep up inside her sensitive flesh. His head was hot, his mouth working, gasping, and a tumultuous eruption was growing, growing in his scrotum ... and from the way Jessie was reacting, he thought she might also be on the verge of climaxing.

Too soon, he thought, too soon ...

On the verge, on the very crest of his orgasm, Bolanger felt Jessie pull away slightly, perfectly timing and tapering off, no more ready to end their ecstasy than he. For a long moment longer her mouth lightly suckled his thickened shaft, her tongue dancing teasingly on its bulbous tip. Then she pivoted up, squatting over him, astride him, knees on the bed on either side of his hips.

She gazed down at him with eyes filmed with passion, and then impaled herself on his spearing erection, contracting her strong inner thighs, her muscular action clamping her moist passage tightly around his shaft. "You like?"

"I like," Bolanger groaned, thrusting his hips up off the covers in greedy response. "Oh, I like . . ."

Jessie splayed her kneeling legs, settling down until she contained all of his rigid, lust-hardened shaft within her. Slowly at first, then with increasing fierceness, she began sliding up and down. Her head sagged, then tautened again in arousal, a vein standing out at the side of her throat with the fury of her pumping exertion. Her mouth opened and closed in mute testimony to the exquisite sensations plundering her loins, her long blond hair swaying and brushing down over her shoulders and across his chest.

Bolanger grasped her jiggling breasts, toying harshly with them until hoarse moans were drawn from her slackened lips. She bent for a brief moment with a whisper of a kiss, then arched up and back as she plunged deeper, faster, reaching behind to caress Bolanger's scrotum, massaging with delicately stroking fingernails. The backward angle made her body toss precariously on Bolanger's hips, her thighs descending with building force, only to reverse at the last instant and draw up again on his penetrating shaft.

Bolanger, tensing upward, felt the gripping of her sheath tearing at his entrails. "God, Jessie, you're like a vise," he panted.

Her passage kept squeezing, squeezing, as she crooned above him, her mouth open, her eyes wide and sightless. The squeezing grew unbearable until, bursting, Bolanger came again. Jessie's loins worked and sucked as if his juices were some invigorating tonic, to be ravenously swallowed in her belly, as her face contorted and twisted with spasming climax.

Then, with an ebb of passion, Jessie crouched, limp and satiated, over Bolanger. Slowly, sighing contentedly, she eased off his flaccid body and lay down on the bed alongside him. Bolanger felt drugged, unable to move. He wanted to say something, but was at a loss for words. Instead he silently cradled her in his arms and dozed off, their bodies remaining loosely entwined.

Chapter 8

Jessie knew by his expression that Police Chief Weims was more hurt than angry. He said so, and his raw-beef face wore an expression of saddened disillusion.

"Seems like you might've come to me first, Miz Starbuck." He sighed. "It ain't hardly fair to expect us cops to catch your heisters when the papers have given 'em a head start."

"I don't expect you to catch them," Jessie said. "I'm surprised that you're even pretending to look." Actually, she was not surprised. The chief couldn't very well do anything else, with the *News-Dispatch* carrying the story in banner headlines. She had seen to that herself. After leaving Bolanger at dawn, she had driven the grocery wagon to the Metropole, where she had awakened Ki and filled him in on the situation, and then they had gone to the newspaper. The editor and reporters, already aware of her abduction off a city street in broad daylight, went wild interviewing her and photographing the wagon with the body of Pocker in back. Other than keeping Bolanger out of it, she told them a straight story, and what with her condition, her chemise and everything else as evidence, nobody doubted her word.

When the reporters had asked her what she intended to do now, she'd replied, "I'm going to sit in my hotel room till you fellows have made me famous enough so it's safe for me to walk around." And that had been accomplished, just as soon as the paper's next edition hit the streets.

"You keep hinting around," the chief complained. "If you have anything on your chest, why don't you come out and say so?"

"Listen, I've tried leveling with you, and what has it got me? Yesterday morning I gave you a dozen better candidates for the killing of District Attorney Emerson than Mrs. Whitworth. Did you do anything about them—except maybe send Alderman Churlak around to warn us off? Today I give you accurate descriptions of Leo, Marie, and where her cabin is located, and what are you doing about them? Your idea is that they're just local riffraff who tried a kidnapping for a few easy bucks." She smiled thinly. "Somebody made a slip, Chief. He's going to make others. If I were you, I'd get out from under."

Weims licked his lips. "You're suggesting what?"

"You ought to know who you're taking orders from better than I do."

Weims thrust out a bulldog jaw. "I don't like that, Miz Starbuck. Nobody's giving me the kind of orders you're hinting at."

"Hinting—*Lord!*" Jessie took a deep breath. "All right, say you're average honest. That leaves you just plain stupid if you can't see that somebody wanted Emerson out of the way and used Whitworth and Whitworth's wife—yes, and me—to make the case complete."

Something glowed far back in the chief's bloodshot eyes. "Give me a name, Miz Starbuck. Give me something to hang my hat on."

104

"I've given you three—Pocker, Leo, and Marie. For a start, pick up the two who're missing and find out what names they know."

"Don't think we won't. I've got lines out, and something's liable to pop anytime now." He moved his ungainly bulk over to Jessie's hotel-room window, glanced out, then stared over at Ki, who was sitting quietly in an armchair near the door. "I understand you two dropped in to see Ike Temple yesterday afternoon."

Jessie nodded.

"And visited Thurlow Dobbs's bank. Then there's your solo trip out to see Emerson's widow. You call that leveling with me, Miz Starbuck?"

"I told you Mrs. Emerson was a better bet than Mrs. Whitworth. You didn't seem to want to believe it, so I went out to have a chat with her myself. As for Mr. Temple, he's in the real estate business. Cyrene Yarbrough is living in a leased house. I thought maybe I could get a line on her through him. And besides, I saw a friend of yours watching the place."

Weims's red neck grew redder. "That suggest anything to you?"

"Maybe."

"But not that I might be after the same thing as you are?"

Jessie regarded him with speculative eyes. "If I wished to be nasty, I could say that you, better than anyone else, seem to know where I was practically every minute of the day."

"Meaning I sent Leo and Pocker after you myself?"

"I didn't say I wished to be nasty."

"Well, what do you wish?"

"Whitworth's killer."

"That all?"

"And Mrs. Whitworth's."

"You haven't proved that she's dead yet."

"I've told you where to look for her."

Weims's shoulders sagged. "All right, we're going to look."

"Then everything's fine, isn't it?"

"Sure," Weims said sarcastically. "You and the Reform Council have put me in one awful spot, that's what you've done. I produce the impossible or I'm thrown out on my a— thrown out."

There was a knock on the door, and a detective entered. He crossed to the chief, trying to smooth out his rumpled suit, and whispered a message into the chief's ear. Surprise and pleasure were mirrored on Weims's florid face as he listened. He said, "yeah, yeah," a couple of times, then, "Okay. Don't do anything else until I get there." He waited until the detective had left the room and the door was shut before turning to Jessie and Ki. "Some of the boys think they got your pals bottled up. Want to go out and watch us do our duty?"

"Why not?" Jessie said. Accompanied by Ki, she went downstairs with Chief Weims and out to a black police surrey with a uniformed man at the reins. They headed easterly, away from the downtown and Lake Michigan, and turned onto a well-used wagon road that more or less paralleled the Illinois and Michigan Canal. Soon they were past the built-up area and moving along at a fast clip through rolling countryside. Jessie asked, "What makes you think you've got them sewed up?"

"I told you we had lines out," Weims said. "A stoolie recognized the descriptions and started nosing around. He made out the couple in a gin joint near the stockyards, but by the time the boys got the tip and got over there the couple had stolen horses and lammed." He chuckled. "They lammed, okay, lammed right into a barricade across the Canal Pikeway, turned tail and beat it back toward town, ran into some more opposition and took a detour. The detour don't go no place. We got 'em penned in a rim of rocks that a lizard couldn't get out of without being seen."

"You're sure they're Leo and Marie?"

"Uh-huh. Leo Hackette and Marie 'Sweet Mama' Goldstein. The dead guy you heard called Pocker got identified as Hercule Pockerlassitow. If I had a name like that, I'd want to be called Pocker, too."

"Local?"

"Never heard of any of 'em," Weims said cheerfully.

"Then you wouldn't know who they were working for?"

Some of the chief's good humor leaked away. "Do they have to be working for somebody?" He eased his bulk into a more comfortable position on the seat, bracing himself as the surrey turned off on a side trail. "Look, a well-dressed lady comes out of a bank with a bodyguard. Even guys with names like Pockerlassitow might guess she was carrying money, or could lay her hands on plenty, so soon's she's on her lonesome, they pick her up for an easy score."

"You keep pushing that idea at me as if maybe I'll swallow it."

"Well, you got a better one?"

"Pocker and Leo are just a pair of simpleminded lads with single-track minds, is that it? They figure out a foolproof technique, rope in Marie, and stick to it." Jessie pursed her lips. "I wonder what bank Millicent Whitworth was coming out of—at midnight."

"Oh, that again!"

Ahead, three or four wagons and a number of saddle horses were clustered at the shoulder of the trail. Chief Weims's driver reined in and parked the wagon behind them. A man in plainclothes and three uniformed officers came up. "This ain't going to be as easy as it looked, Chief. One of 'em just winged Gahagan."

107

Weims stifled a curse. "I thought I ordered you to hold off till we got here."

"You should have told Leo Hackette, too," the cop said.

Off to the right, around a bend in the trail that followed the bottom of a shallow gulch, gunshots split the day wide open. Stung into action, repeater carbines opened up. "What are you trying to do," Jessie said, "catch them or blast the rocks down on top of them?"

The plainclothesman looked at her. He was the cop who had been working with Detective Brody the day before. "Maybe they'll talk to you, lady. They didn't seem to want to talk to us."

Weims cleared his throat. "Well, what are we waiting for?" He lumbered along the rutted trail. Jessie, Ki, and the plainclothesman followed him, while the uniformed cops stayed behind with the horses and wagons. There were no more shots.

Around the bend they came to a steep hillside cluttered with rocks and stunted brush. Some of the rocks screened men, obviously cops. Above them, under the overhang of a cliff, more rocks made a parapet around a shallow depression, and it was presumably in this natural bowl that the quarry had taken refuge. As if to prove this assumption, a half-dozen carbines fired a rapid volley of shots at the parapet. Off to the left and higher up the slope there was an answering chatter of rifle and pistol fire.

Weims's voice was a hoarse whisper in Jessie's ear. "Trying to suck them into using up their ammunition." A chunk of lead smacked into the rock beside him. He fell down behind it and began crawling on his belly toward another, larger rock. "Find your own shade, Miz Starbuck!"

Quite suddenly Jessie was frightened. She could not have explained why exactly, but she was frightened.

She glanced at Ki, then looked around for the chief, but couldn't find him. It occurred to her that she and Ki were in a fine spot to catch slugs from anyone who didn't happen to like them. With all this lead flying about, who would be able to say they hadn't been hit accidentally?

She dove with Ki at a clump of brush just as the carbines opened up again. It seemed to her that the place she had just left was filled with the sound of angry hornets. She lay perfectly still, waiting for the racket to subside, wishing she had a gun.

"You okay, Miz Starbuck?" Weims yelled. "How about your bodyguard?"

"We're okay," Jessie said. Motioning to Ki, she rolled swiftly away from her inadequate shelter. Nobody tried to cut the clump of brush to bits. Breathing unevenly, she attained the sanctuary of a boulder the size of a small house; Ki slid in close alongside her. They sat with their backs to the rock, knees drawn up, watching the cluttered slope around them. Nothing moved within their range of vision, nothing at all.

After a while, and even farther away now, the chief's voice was lifted in a shout. "Hey you! Hackette! Sweet Mama!"

The couple in the little rock fortress were not very talkative. A shot answered him, then another. This provoked an indignant reply from the carbines. None of the bullets seemed to be looking for Jessie or Ki. Jessie let out her breath, slowly.

"That ain't gonna do you no good!" Weims yelled. "You two gonna play nice, or shall we toss some black powder sticks in to keep you company?"

There was no answer.

"OK, you asked for it!" Apparently one of the cops had worked up close to the parapet with a cannister of explosive, for undercovering fire from other cops lower down, he suddenly reared and pitched the can over the top, then ducked and ran down the slope. A second ... two seconds ... then the powder exploded, the bouldered crest of the hill erupting high into the sky. The concussion was deafening, hurtling thick, belching clouds of smoke and rocky debris over the parapet and cops below. There were muffled curses, a hacking, tearing cough; then, like wraiths, like genies conjured up by the smoke, two dim figures took shape and a woman's voice sobbed, "Okay, we're—"

A premonition of what was about to happen seized Jessie, and she stood up, yelling, "Don't, don't! Stay where you are!"

Something that could have been a bee but wasn't sung past her ear, ricocheted from the outcropping, and went screaming off. There was the sound of a shot. Then the carbines ripped open furiously. Then it was still again. Flat on her belly, Jessie stared with sickened eyes at the slope, at the piled-up rocks on which lay two dark splotches, twisted and inert under the pall of powder smoke.

Men were walking toward them now, upright and without hurry, for they were no longer dangerous. Especially they were not dangerous to the one who had hired them. Leo Hackette and Marie 'Sweet Mama' Goldstein, like Hercule Pockerlassitow, were all through talking ...

Promptly at four o'clock that afternoon, a coroner's jury was asked to consider testimony in the matter of the death by violence of one Harold Whitworth, general manager of Starbuck Purveyors. The jury, five men and one woman, tried to look interested, but they obviously resented being kept from whatever they had intended doing that afternoon. The coroner was a round-faced, well-fed man with a pince-nez and a brisk, efficient manner that said his time was important.

An enormous fly with green wings buzzed angrily about the room, banging against the walls, the windows. Jessie, beside Ki in the third row of hard, stiff-back chairs, gloomily likened the fly to herself. The fly was trying, but wasn't getting anywhere.

The coroner's physician and the police autopsy surgeon both certified the cause of death as three bullets, entering the heart, right lung, and lower abdomen of the deceased. That seemed to dispose of the fact that Harold Whitworth was dead, which everybody had known in the first place.

The coroner cleared his throat. "Miss Jessica Starbuck."

Jessie rose, pushed past the knees of people between her and the aisle, and took the chair. In response to direct questioning, she said yes, she had been the employer of the deceased. She thought she looked pretty good, considering. She had on a gray-green two-piece suit, a white silk blouse, and a darker green hat. The color scheme was interestingly carried out in the bruise on her right cheekbone.

"Was the deceased pursuing any other line of work at the time of his death?"

"I wouldn't know," Jessie said. "I wasn't here at the time of his death."

The coroner looked annoyed. "That isn't what I meant. Was he engaged in Chicago in any other capacity than as manager of your packing company?"

"Not to my certain knowledge. If you want hearsay—" Jessie looked at Mrs. Emerson, beside her father in the first row of chairs. She was more attractive than when Jessie had seen her the day before; Judge Nichol looked as though he hadn't slept very well.

The coroner said they better stick to the facts. "Have you any idea where we can find Mrs. Whitworth?"

"Sorry, no," Jessie said. She was dismissed.

The bank officer, Gregory Boothroyd, took the stand next. He gave Jessie and Ki a dirty look, erased that, and preened himself for the benefit of the spectators. Yes, he had viewed the remains and was willing to swear that the deceased was the same man who had tried to bribe him into divulging information.

"About what?"

Boothroyd was very conscious of Jessie's stare. To Jessie he had admitted actually selling the information to Whitworth. To the police and his employers he had denied all but the approach. He concentrated on his shoes. "Mr. Whitworth wanted to know the condition of District Attorney Emerson's account."

"But you didn't tell him?"

"N-no."

"You've since learned that the account is practically exhausted?"

"That's rather common knowledge, isn't it?" Boothroyd was on safer ground now. The police, acting on his information about Whitworth, had interrogated officials of the Illinois National Bank.

"Thank you, Mr. Boothroyd." The coroner rustled his papers. "Chief of Police Weims."

Weims took the witness chair. He looked smug and self-satisfied, as befitted a man whose department had functioned so efficiently in the matter of Leo and Marie. All you had to do, his manner said, was give him something he could sink his teeth into. Justice would follow, swift and sure. Questioned, he said that he and his men had been unable to find any evidence of Whitworth's activities other than the inquiry about Emerson. He could give no reason even for that.

The coroner next called Mrs. Emerson. "Believe me, this is as distasteful to me as it must be to you, madam." The coroner took off his glasses and polished them absently. "Have you any knowledge as to why the deceased should have been interested in your husband?"

Behind her black veil Mrs. Emerson's face was composed. "No."

"Thank you. I believe that's all."

The jury was out less than two minutes. It returned with a verdict of willful murder against party or parties unknown. Jessie surmised that the foreman knew, and his fellows, and everybody else in Chicago, that District Attorney Emerson had shot Whitworth, but what the hell? Whitworth's wife had shot Emerson, hadn't she? So that made it even, and what was the use of embarrassing a nice-looking widow like Mrs. Emerson?

After the inquest, Jessie checked with the telegraph office for messages from the Circle Star, then met briefly with Thurlow Dobbs to obtain the banking information he had collected for her. She and Ki ate a quiet dinner and retired early.

Next morning, skipping breakfast, they drove their rental buggy out to a particular spot along Lake Michigan. When they arrived, the could see bright sunlight reflecting off the lake waters, hampering the cops in the steam launch who were fooling around with grappling hooks. On the shore nearest them extended a short pier, with a path curving up from the shore into a grove of trees beyond. On the far side of the grove, the path wound across a field to a wagon road—the road that went past Marie Goldstein's cabin a short distance away.

Ki parked the buggy on the bank up by the grove. While he was tethering the horse in a shady patch of grass, Jessie laid out a large plaid blanket and emptied a wicker hamper. They settled on the blanket and enjoyed a picnic brunch, repleat with chicken sandwiches and a bottle of chilled wine.

Relaxing after his fourth sandwich, Ki shaded his eyes against the glare with the newspaper he had been reading. "Well, Jessie? What've you deduced from all the facts and figures our roly-poly friend gave you?"

"You mean good ol' Thurlow Dobbs, the people's pal?" Jessie smiled and sipped her wine. "Judge Nichol's account seems to be the only one that's noticeably fattened of late. Ike Temple shows a small net loss. If you can believe their bank accounts, Weims, Churlak, and even Ruben Garibaldi are all honest men. Of course, they can all have accounts somewhere else. All except Weims have safety deposit boxes."

"Then Dobbs's information accomplishes nothing?"

"Oh, I wouldn't say that. It proves Dobbs expected me to be around to ask for it."

"You suspect him?"

"It was just up the street from his bank that I got nabbed," Jessie noted. "I learned something else. Somebody had been bleeding Emerson before he moved his account to Illinois National. Ever since his election, in fact."

"Meaning that if he were crooked, he wasn't making any money at it," Ki said. "To me, the whole thing resolves into this: Harold Whitworth wasn't involved long enough to learn much more than we have, Jessie. Therefore, his death wasn't necessary except as a means of getting rid of Emerson. Presumably, then, he was led to join the council for that express purpose, and I'm damned if I can see why *that* was necessary. I think maybe I should have another talk with the brunette."

Jessie laughed once, sharply. "Another all-night talk?"

"I'm serious," Ki said, poker-faced. "Mrs. Emerson says her husband claimed he was cultivating Cyrene Yarbrough in search of evidence, right? Maybe he found some. Maybe that's why he was killed."

"Maybe so." Jessie nodded, her eyes brooding on the vista of Lake Michigan under the sunlight. If it hadn't been for lust and luck, she herself would be out there, being eaten by the fishes. She couldn't figure the reason for that, exactly. Perhaps someone had just thought she might find out something, and the opportunity to get rid of her was too good to pass up. She tended to agree with Ki's assessment: Whitworth had been lured into this as part of an engineered scheme to eliminate Emerson, who was supposed to kill Whitworth and then get killed in reprisal. Emerson's killer would then vanish, and the case would be allowed to die a natural death. If nothing else, the inquest yesterday had proved how nearly the mastermind had been able to gauge public opinion. Unconscious that she was speaking aloud, Jessie said, "What mastermind?"

"I'll take Garibaldi," Ki decided. "If he and his family are running the crime operations hereabouts, like everybody says, then he'd be the one paying off the cops and officials, the one behind everything with everything to lose."

"Or Alderman Churlak," Jessie suggested. "Weims is part of his faction. It could be that after I got away, Leo and Marie made contact and were told to lay low. After all, why would they have stuck around Chicago all night if they hadn't been ordered to? It was a setup—the order then came to scram out of town, the idea being that the cops would get itchy trigger fingers and there wouldn't be any more loose ends to embarrass people. We saw it happen, Ki. And in the process, maybe we were meant to stop a stray bullet or two."

"There must've been thirty cops out on that hillside. Any one of them could've been potting at us." Ki scowled. "Weims claims it was Leo and Marie. He says anyway it was all our fault, going to the papers instead of keeping the thing hush-hush." Ki grinned teasingly.

"Tell you what, while I'm talking to the brunette, why don't you talk with Garibaldi and Churlak? All you've got to do is ask them, and I bet they'll admit they did it." Abruptly he lost his grin and straightened, hearing horses slowly approaching from the grove. "Speak of the devil . . ."

Not turning, Jessie said stiffly, "Who is it?"

"Garibaldi."

"Alone?"

"He has a couple of his sons with him."

With a low sigh, Jessie leaned back and closed her eyes, tightly, in the belief that if she couldn't see what was coming she wouldn't mind it so much. She heard the creak of saddle leather as the men dismounted, then the soft tread of their boots as they walked to the wagon.

"Hello, Miss Starbuck, Ki." Garibaldi's gravelly voice held a hint of amusement.

Jessie opened her eyes with a fine show of astonishment. Garibaldi was looming over her, hands clasped behind his back. His sons were a respectful distance away.

"If you're afeard, Miss Starbuck, no need to be."

Jessie grew indignant. "No? You read the papers, don't you? People dying like flies around here and you ask me if I'm frightened?"

"You don't think I've had anything to do with that, do you?"

"How would I know?" A bit recklessly she added, "Leo Hackette and Pocker knew you, all right. I told them I was a friend of yours, but they didn't seem to believe it."

"What else did they have to say?"

"Nothing. They were having too fine a time to talk much." She pointed her forefinger at Garibaldi. "You think if they'd told me anything—and I could prove it on you—I wouldn't have told the paper?"

"But it's in your mind," Garibaldi insisted, and when Jessie said nothing to that: "I was afraid it might be. In fact some of my own boys have kind of got the idea that I sent 'em on the job and then tossed 'em to the cops afterwards." He grimaced. "That kind of thing is bad for business."

"I can see how it would be," Jessie admitted. "What do you want me to do—announce that it wasn't you who hired them?" She shrugged. "Give me the name of a more likely prospect and maybe I will."

Garibaldi considered that carefully. "So I am a likely prospect. Why should I give a damn one way or another?"

"Why was Harold Whitworth killed?"

"I'll bite. Why?"

"He's supposed to have been investigating Emerson, who was supposed to have turned out no better than his predecessor. Even at its face value, it means that someone needed protection." Jessie lifted a hand as Garibaldi was about to say something. "Politicians have been known to switch sides before—especially if the stench becomes too bad for even the voters to miss."

Not a muscle in Garibaldi's face moved. After a moment he asked casually, "Think they'll find anything out there?"

"Do you?"

"No."

"Neither do I," Jessie said. "Chief Weims is giving me a play, just as he did with Leo and Marie yesterday."

"No cop likes to admit he can't handle his own territory." Garibaldi appeared to be turning something over in his mind. "About Hackette and Pocker—they weren't my boys. They'd pulled a job in Cicero and were hotter than firecrackers when they asked me to hide them out."

117

"Whatever you say. Am I arguing?"

"P'r'aps not, but what're you trying to prove?"

"That Millicent Whitworth is innocent."

Garibaldi narrowed his raisin eyes. "You must have a darn good notion that she ain't out there in the lake after all. Otherwise, you wouldn't be so eager to clear her."

Jessie gave him a tight-lipped grin. "She's out there, I'm afraid. Leo and Pocker tried to put me beside her, remember?"

Garibaldi nodded. "Well, I'll be seeing you at the inquest." Briskly he turned away, joined his sons, and together they trooped back to the horses.

Jessie watched them ride off. "I think I'll be sick . . ."

Around noon the second coroner's jury was convened, and for this occasion the jury was all men. They looked hand-picked. This was no routine inquiry into the death of some unknown citizen; nope, this had to do with one of their leading dignitaries and a duly elected officer of the law. Most of the spectators seemed to feel the same way; such looks as were cast in Jessie's direction were not exactly hostile, but she had the distinct impression that as the employer of Millicent Whitworth's husband, she was suspected of complicity in the killing of District Attorney Emerson. Chief Weims's notable lack of success in finding Millicent's body in Lake Michigan seemed to have convinced everybody that she wasn't there—that it was, somehow, all a ruse on Jessie's part to have instigated the search in the first place.

Thurlow Dobbs, Ike Temple, and Judge Nichol formed a protective shell about Mrs. Emerson. It was patent that they were there to insulate her against any hint of scandal, and also to mark down in their little black books any witness who might dare to testify except in her behalf. Carefully separated from them by the width of the packed room, Ruben Garibaldi and his sons sat and talked together in low tones. In the very front row of chairs was the dapper Alderman Churlak, Chief Weims, and a police surgeon.

Again the first witnesses called were the surgeon and the coroner's physician. They testified as to the exact cause of death, the time of death, the condition of the body when it was first discovered. Next up was Chief Weims, who waddled importantly to the chair. The coroner fixed Weims with a stare that seemed intended to be read as impartial, and asked him to tell what he knew.

Weims addressed himself to the loudly ticking clock on the far wall. "Well ..." He recounted getting the report, his subsequent arrival at the crime scene, and seeing the body clad in pajamas and dressing robe, lying in the lower hall of the house. From the condition of Emerson's bed, it seemed that the district attorney had retired, but apparently risen again, possibly to answer the door. No one had heard the door bell or any knocking. The shots themselves had awakened the maid and Mrs. Emerson. There had been no sign of the murder weapon in the house or around the grounds.

The coroner asked, "And your conclusions?"

"I've been trying to locate a Mrs. Millicent Whitworth." Weims caught Jessie's eye and added hastily, "For questioning."

"You think she is implicated?"

"She had a motive—sort of." Weims carefully avoided looking at Jessie again. "The bank officer coming forward and all, and ... well, when we went to look for her, she'd run out on us. We later established that she had had a gun. According to her husband's employer, Miss Starbuck, she'd taken it away, but—"

Jessie stood up. "May I ask the chief a question?"

The coroner glared at her. Everybody glared at her. "You will be called next, Miss Starbuck." The coroner waited until Jessie sat back down, then asked Weims, "Didn't Miss Starbuck turn this gun over to you?"

Weims colored. "She turned *a* gun over to me."

"You mean the gun wasn't registered to Mrs. Whitworth?"

Weims mopped his brow with a handkerchief. "Well, sure, but . . ." Without saying it, he implied that Millicent could have gotten another gun.

"Miss Jessica Starbuck!"

They went through the preliminary questions and answers. Interrogated about the gun, Jessie answered yes, she had taken it away from Mrs. Whitworth, who was naturally upset over her husband's murder. Jessie was afraid she'd commit suicide.

"You didn't see her again that night—or since then?"

"No."

"Then you can't swear that it *wasn't* her who did unto death the deceased Lewis Emerson?"

"No."

"I think that will be all, Miss Starbuck."

"No."

The coroner gaped. "I beg your pardon?"

"No," Jessie insisted. "Listen, since much of the evidence so far introduced has been rather inimical to Mrs. Whitworth, I think it's only fair to point out that there's another lady who had a motive for shooting the district attorney, a lady who also had a gun."

Judge Nichol's eyes hated her, but then so did Ike Temple's and the ordinarily merry eyes of banker Dobbs. Only Alderman Churlak kept his professional politico's smile. Jessie pointed a dramatic finger at Chief Weims's bulbous nose and declared:

"Here's my question. Have you compared the bullets taken from Emerson's body with the one fired in Garibaldi's Old Lompoc House the other night?"

For an instant there was complete silence in the room. Then somebody sneezed and pandemonium broke loose. Jessie thought what a hell of a fine target she made, sitting there in the witness chair. She tried to watch Weims, Garibaldi, and his sons all at the same time, but it was a little difficult because they were so far apart.

Mrs. Emerson quietly fainted.

A matron called in from the adjoining jail helped Judge Nichol revive his daughter. Restored to consciousness, her face a white mask behind the heavy black-bordered veil, Mrs. Emerson refused to leave the courtroom. She resumed the seat beside her father.

The coroner rapped sharply for order. "That's all very unusual," he said to no one in particular, then eyed Weims. "You heard Miss Starbuck's query."

Weims muttered that he'd heard. "I didn't attach any importance to it at the time."

"You didn't attach any importance to what?"

"Well, I, er . . . I guess I kind of forgot about that shooting in Garibaldi's. Nobody got hurt and I . . ." He shot an appealing glance at Alderman Churlak, took a deep breath, and admitted he hadn't recovered the bullet fired there. He wouldn't even know where to look. It was obvious that he hoped it had gone out a window.

The coroner stared hard at Jessie. "Perhaps you can help us."

"Yes," Jessie said. "It's buried in the carpet under Mrs. Emerson's table at her home. There are a couple of reporters over there now with their feet on it."

Mrs. Emerson stood up, eluded her father's restraining hand, and moved straight and tall and proud into the aisle. "Very well," she said in a perfectly calm voice. "I shot my husband. He deserved it so I shot him."

There was nothing the coroner's jury could do but recommend that she be detained.

Chapter 9

There was a lady in Ki's hotel room. Beside her on the settee were her gloves, bag, and a broad-brimmed hat with a small crown that made a splash of Mandarin red, matching a tailored suit of what looked like red serge. Because her feet were propped comfortably on a chair and the hem of her skirt was riding high, Ki got a provocative view of firm legs above her ankle boots.

He said, "Mmm, I bet you've got red undies on, too." His eyes expressed no surprise at finding her there in his room. As he closed the door, he thought she would probably get around to telling him about it when she was good and ready.

With daylight makeup her mouth was no longer the imperious scarlet slash. "You've been rather conspicuously ignoring me lately, darling. I'm not used to that."

His manner became earnest. "You think I like it? I've been busy."

She nodded. "I've heard." She withdrew her feet from the chair, crossed her knees, and settled herself more primly on the settee. "Ruben doesn't like Miss Starbuck very well for lighting fires to see what boils—like mentioning that shooting at his place."

"What did he expect her to do—sit there and let them smear a woman who wasn't around to defend herself? Garibaldi send you around?"

She shook her head. "Nobody sends Cyrene Yarbrough anyplace, darling. I just thought you should know he isn't liking either of you too much. He thinks the customers are liable to stay away from a place where such things happen."

"It wasn't exactly a secret anyway," Ki pointed out.

"No," she agreed. Dark lashes lay heavily against her cheeks. "Still, it could've been forgotten. There are other things that could be forgotten, too."

Ki thought of Alderman Churlak's not-too-subtle threat. "Such as my alibi for the time Emerson was killed?"

She shrugged. "No woman likes scandal, Ki. Especially after she's lied like a lady for a man."

"You didn't lie. I was there."

"Were you, darling?" Her mouth drooped. "At first I thought you were a heel for telling the police you spent the night with me. Then I saw that it was necessary and I forgave you."

He became indignant. "I don't need your forgiving. I don't give a damn. You can't play me for a sucker like you do the rest of them." And then, as if ashamed of his hard stance, he said, "Actually, I was going to drop in on you tonight."

"Oh?"

"I wanted to ask you a few things. Emerson was cultivating you and ended up with a couple of slugs in his chest. So Jessie—Miss Starbuck—and I meet you and what does it draw us? She's almost killed and I'm suspected of murder." He leaned and grasped her roughly by the shoulders. "I want to know if there's any connection." Her eyes were deep wells in which he easily could have lost himself. "Who sent you up here, Cyrene? Ike Temple? Judge Nichol? Come to think of it, it was Churlak who suggested you might be persuaded to leave me out on a limb, so they could hook me and spring Mrs. Emerson." He saw her eyes narrow slightly. "Go ahead and play with whoever it is you're playing with, but don't forget what happened to Sweet Mama Goldstein. She played, too."

Cyrene stood up. "I've nothing to fear, Ki."

"Okay, you've nothing to fear. Say you're a little sore at me and willing to do another guy a favor—like saying sure, I visited your home but didn't actually sleep with you, so maybe I could've shot Emerson. How long do you think it will be before this guy gets worrying about whether you'll stick to your story? Especially if he's hot for Mrs. Emerson?" Ki saw calculation come into her eyes. He put both arms around her and kissed her, hard. "Be smart, Cyrene."

She freed herself. "What are you after, Ki?"

"You."

She shook her head. "No, I don't mean that."

He was breathing unevenly, and it was not all pretense that the kiss had left him shaken. He said, "All right, I want Whitworth's killer, just like Miss Starbuck does. You can help us get him."

Her lips scarcely moved. "Emerson killed him."

"You and I know better than that."

"Yes, I imagine we do. Maybe I can help you. I don't know." In her eyes was uncertainty. "Drop around to the house tonight. Bring Miss Starbuck along, if you wish. I may have something for you."

"If you've got something to spill, spill it now."

"No." Her tone, her manner said that she could be just as stubborn as he. "Perhaps I have something to find out first." Unhurriedly she put on her hat, picked up her gloves and bag. She offered her mouth for his kiss. "Until tonight, darling . . ."

125

After Cyrene Yarbrough left his room, Ki waited a few minutes and then went down the hall to the floor's communal bathroom, washed up, and went downstairs to the dining room. Jessie was already there, seated at a remote corner table, toying with a dinner for which she had no appetite. She brightened as Ki approached, and when he sat down across from her, she said teasingly, "I caught of glimpse of Cyrene Yarbrough going out through the lobby. Lover's spat?"

"She wanted to know why I hadn't been around to see her, so she came up to find out." Pausing as the waiter came by, Ki ordered steak and then continued. "At least that's what she said. Somebody sent her, Jessie. She's invited us over tonight, so maybe we'll find out who, if we play it right."

"Come into my fine parlor, invited the spider to the fly," Jessie murmured. Then, glancing at the dining room entrance, she said, "We've got visitors, uninvited."

Trooping toward their table came Thurlow Dobbs and Judge Nichol. Dobbs had a newspaper folded under one arm and, seeming to have forgotten his momentary displeasure with Jessie, was again his jovial self. Nichol's feelings were carefully masked behind a reserved, polite exterior. "May I speak to you a moment, Miss Starbuck?"

"Of course."

Nichol seemed to have some trouble framing his next words. Finally he said in his precise, unemotional voice, "You don't really believe my daughter shot her husband, do you?"

"I didn't say she did."

"You implied it."

Jessie shook her head. "I just remembered something that everyone else appeared to have forgotten."

Color dyed Nichol's cheeks. "I put it to you that you had never lost sight of that unfortunate incident in the Old Lompoc. You were merely saving it for what you considered the most auspicious moment. I want to know why."

"This is all beside the point, isn't it? What I did or when I did it has nothing to do with the facts as they're now established. No matter what I said now, it wouldn't alter the facts. The only solution that I can see is for you to find a more logical suspect to take your daughter's place."

"I see," Nichol said. Briefly his eyes were those of a man not only capable of killing, but of finding a deal of satisfaction in it. "Maybe it will come to that, Miss Starbuck. Maybe I shall have to do that very—"

"Marvin!" Thurlow Dobbs interposed his bulk between the judge and Jessie. "We're trying to enlist Miss Starbuck's assistance, not antagonize her." Turning, he took the paper from under his arm and handed it to Jessie. "Latest edition. The bullets matched. You rather expected that, didn't you?"

"I'm surprised the police ever let the bullets reach the comparison microscope," Jessie replied, somewhat sarcastically. "I repeat, it isn't what I expect or think or say that counts. It's proof that's wanted, and there isn't anything here that someone with a garden spade couldn't turn up—if he had the time and the inclination."

"And top authority," Judge Nichol said.

"Your Civic Reform Council has top authority over a good part of Lake Michigan. Why don't you look for Mrs. Whitworth?"

"I don't know for sure that you were due to be thrown in."

"Don't tell me I dreamt up Pocker and Leo Hackette, too!"

"They were fugitives anyway, Miss Starbuck, due to a holdup in Cicero."

"All right, just forget the whole thing."

Dobbs sighed, gently. "I can see why you're the head of the Starbuck organization. You're not the easiest young woman to get along with. What would you say if I told you Judge Nichol intended to confess to the killing himself?"

"I'd say he better not leave any loopholes in his story, then," Jessie replied, and looked very hard at the judge. "Because even Chief Weims has sense enough to figure you might try such a move to spring your daughter."

With a terse "G'day," Nichol stalked off. Thurlow Dobbs was a little more gracious, but departed a step behind the judge. And that was that.

Shortly after dark, around eight-thirty, Jessie and Ki checked out their rental buggy from the livery and rode over to visit Cyrene Yarbrough. Approaching her leased house, Ki was about to rein in when they spotted a saddle horse tied to the hitch post in front of her porch. There were lights on in the house, though none showed in either of its nearest neighbors. That meant, almost certainly, that whoever owned the horse was inside Cyrene's house, closeted with the brunette.

With a flick of the reins, Ki guided the buggy on past. Against the pale translucency of closed Brussels lace curtains, they thought they saw the shadow of a man outlined briefly; then it was gone and the window itself was gone, and they were looking around for a place to park the buggy where it wouldn't stick out like a sore thumb.

When presently they found it, they were a good hundred yards beyond the house, and there were two other houses intervening between them and it. Ki reined the buggy hard around and halted it in a sort of tunnel between a tall hedge bordering an estate and the trees lining the street. They got out and began backtracking on foot, and were less than twenty feet from the house when the front door opened and the figure of a man was silhouetted against the light from within. Jessie would have recognized that silhouette anywhere. It belonged to the lean, ungainly Ike Temple.

Then the closing door blotted the man out, and for an instant it was like grasping a handful of smoke, trying to pick him up again among the shadows that lay so heavily across the road. Jessie and Ki had scarcely accomplished this when the figure paused, whirled, and retraced his way to the front door. Keys jingled in the stillness; a lock clicked. Then the door opened and closed, was opened again almost immediately, and Ike Temple reappeared, this time with a hat.

Jessie stifled a laugh. The guy had forgotten his hat. For a moment this obscured the important thing—the fact that Ike Temple had a key to Cyrene Yarbrough's front door. When the full significance did hit her, Jessie decided that she would have to remember the key, not only afterward, but during the coming interview with the brunette. Temple might have forgotten his gloves, too, or his trousers.

Untying the reins of the horse out front, Temple mounted and headed off at a swift trot, a fleeting shadow among other shadows.

When presently Jessie and Ki approached the house, it was more cautiously than Ike Temple had left it. They did not mount the steps as they might otherwise have done. Instead, they went along the side, between the house itself and a border of flowers, their feet no more than a whisper against the compliant carpet of grass. The windows were dark, shaded, until they got around back to the rear door. Next to the door was a half-open window, and they crossed to it and leaned against the sill, listening. From the room beyond, through a partially open door, came subdued lamplight, enough for them to identify the room immediately before them as the kitchen. Then they saw it.

A woman's foot lay in that narrow path of radiance, stood, vertically on its heel, as though nailed to the floor. Jessie watched it with a kind of macabre intensity, pretending that she expected it to move, though she knew that it would not.

"We must get in there, Ki," she whispered urgently. "If only for a moment."

Testing the rear door, they found it locked. Ki inspected the window. There was no screen on it. Cautiously raising the window, he boosted himself inside and unlatched the door, letting Jessie in. He crossed the kitchen and pushed the door wide open. Jessie gasped, then steeled herself.

Cyrene Yarbrough lay flat on her back in the middle of a blue-and-gold Chinese rug. In her outstretched right hand a scarlet handkerchief made a startling blob of color. Against the white breast of her gown there was another splash of carmine. This one was not a handkerchief. Her eyes were wide open, fixed intently on the ceiling.

Kneeling beside her, Jessie laid the back of her hand against a waxen cheek. There was no need for silly business like feeling for a pulse; she had seen enough of death to recognize it when she saw it. The brunette's flesh was cool to the touch, but not cold. "A half hour," she estimated, "possibly an hour."

"I wonder what Ike Temple was doing all that time," Ki said thoughtfully, "just standing around wishing he hadn't done it?"

The weapon, a gun of fairly big caliber to judge from the size of the hole, was not in evidence. Jessie stood up and joined Ki in examining the front room. They saw the reason for Temple's delayed departure: a rifled escritoire, the bookshelves on either side of the fireplace practically denuded. They found the bedroom in even more disorder, "really taken apart," Ki remarked.

Returning to the front room, intent on leaving by the rear, kitchen door, they were startled by footsteps on the front porch and the jiggling of a key in the front-door lock. They hastened out the rear door as the front door swung open. By the glow of the front-room lamp, Jessie caught a glimpse of a plump, elderly woman wearing an apron and head bandanna and taking the key out of the lock. Halfway back to their buggy, they heard the woman scream bloody murder.

Twenty minutes later they were in Jessie's hotel room.

Twenty minutes after that, they were joined by Chief Weims, half a dozen uniformed patrolmen, and three plainclothes detectives, including the one Ki had struck, named Brody.

"Don't tell me you two have been out tonight, Miss Starbuck?" Weims was not completely successful in masking the hard eagerness in his small eyes. It was obvious that he knew damn well that Jessie and Ki had been out, and that he hoped Jessie would deny it.

"Yes, we were." Jessie watched Detective Brody prowling around the room. She tried to make her voice as casual as the chief's. "Any reason why we shouldn't have been?"

Weims ignored that one. "Where'd you go?"

Jessie wondered if perhaps the woman—a cleaning maid, she guessed—had caught a glimpse of her or Ki or both of them leaving the kitchen. She could think of no other means by which the police could have settled on them so quickly. She shrugged. "Just around."

"Then you ain't heard what's happened?"

"That depends on what's happened," Jessie hedged. Brody worried her, snooping around the way he was; he seemed to be looking for something. "One thing about this town of yours, Chief; there doesn't seem to be a dull moment in it."

"Not since you two blew in, that's a fact," Weims said with a laugh and rubbed his jaw. "You see the Yarbrough brunette tonight?"

Jessie decided that the woman had spotted them, all right. And more than likely the cops had checked with the livery stable, perhaps even located where Ki had parked the buggy. "Maybe."

"She's dead," Weims said.

Jessie pretended a vast surprise. *"No!"*

Turning, Weims scowled at Ki. "And you killed her."

"Sure I did," Ki said. He became elaborately sarcastic. "I always go around murdering my own alibis." He strode across and intercepted Brody, who had finally worked around to Jessie's bureau drawers. "Looking for something?"

"Yeah, but I don't think I'll find it. I think even you are too smart for that," Brody said sourly and slammed the top drawer shut. "This alibi of yours, your alibi for the Emerson kill. You admit you had a motive for that one?"

"No, and I didn't kill him."

Weims responded, "So *you* say."

"So Cyrene Yarbrough said, Chief."

"Only she ain't around no more."

Ki looked at Jessie. "Well, that sure shows what we're up against in Chicago. If an alibi happens to be an inconvenience to them—especially to the daughter of a prominent citizen—they just get rid of the alibi."

"What's this?" Brody cut in, eyes agleam. His hand was rummaging through the clothes in the bottom drawer of the bureau. "There's a gun hidden in here."

132

He brought out the gun and displayed it. "Yours, Miss Starbuck?"

Jessie was a little surprised to see that it was. She had thought it might be Mrs. Emerson's, the one that had been used to kill her husband. Then she realized that this wouldn't have done at all. Even she was supposed to be smarter than to use the gun a second time, for by so doing she would automatically absolve Mrs. Emerson of the first. Mrs. Emerson was in jail. Another killing with the weapon she was accused of firing into her husband's body was bound to spring her. So they'd dug up her custom pistol, which could easily and irrevocably be traced to her. She looked at Weims. "It's mine. It's the one Pocker and Leo Hackette got when they kidnapped me."

"They could hardly have shot Cyrene Yarbrough with it," Weims said, and in a pretense of fairness, added, "Now, there ain't nothing, yet, to prove that this gun is the one used to slay her."

Ki spoke up: "It is, though."

"It is?"

"Naturally. Why else would it be here?"

"So you admit you killed her?"

"Oh, no. I just know a good frame when I see one."

Brody hit him in the mouth. He pressed against Ki, his eyes hot with hate. His coat was open now, and the pistol in his shoulder holster was an invitation. Ki looked past him. The other cops in the room had their guns drawn and were grouping closer. Backing away from Brody, Ki said, "You'd like that, wouldn't you?"

And Brody, shoving forward, snarled, "I don't get it."

Ki sidestepped, glancing at Jessie; she was being held by Weims, his thick hand gripping her tightly by the arm. "You mean I don't get it," Ki said, eyes returning to Brody. "Right here in front of Miss Starbuck and a passel of witnesses." His grin was derisive. "If I'd reached for it, your pals would have nailed me to the wall." He looked at Weims. "I'd like to go on record—"

"You'll go on record, all right," Brody said, and punched Ki in the face again. Responding reflexively, Ki planted the heel of his hand into the center of the detective's face. There was a muffled crunch, and Brody howled, sprawling flat in wild, flailing motions.

His fall acted like a signal to the patrolmen; they barreled in, piling onto Ki, snagging his legs and arms and pistol-whipping him, driving him to the floor. He struggled to rise, both arms gripped tightly by men who hung on and tried to keep him down. Jessie struggled futilely in the grip of Weims and the two patrolmen, unable to help Ki as he was kicked in the ribs and back. Grimly enduring the pain, he battled upright to his knees, then to his feet. He shook off one cop and kidney-punched another in a wildness born of fury and frustration. Another yelp went up; another patrolman went spinning aside and bowling into Brody, who was blearily recovering.

"Shoot him!" Brody raged nasally, his nostrils spurting blood. "No, don't! You're too close! You'll shoot each other!"

Defiantly Ki resisted, managing to dish out some of the considerable savagery of which he was capable. Using elbow smashes, kicks, punches, and openhanded strikes, he brought anguished wails to some and wheezing groans to others, sending them skidding, stumbling, falling to their hands and knees. But there were too many of them, and the odds took their toll. And the gun butts hammered, hammered, hammered at Ki's head with stunning force. Ki felt himself weakening . . . sinking . . . blacking out . . .

Chapter 10

A damp, crawling blackness lay upon his eyelids. Ki could see nothing for a moment, and he had no idea where he was. Every muscle and sinew in his body ached, and though shooting pains of fire darted through his right side when he moved, he managed to turn over and push up onto his knees. His head throbbed from the gun-clubbing he had suffered, and as his senses cleared, he realized his jacket, shirt, and vest had been removed, and everything had been taken from his pants pockets. He heard a man breathing close by and the stir of a shoe on the floor. Then, as his eyes became accustomed to the darkness, he was able to distinguish a set of iron bars that seemed to be suspended in the air in a vertical position.

After a moment he realized that those bars belonged on a cell door. He looked around in the darkness, but could find no window.

The man who was breathing near him stirred again, and then there was a whisper: "Are you awake?"

"Yes," Ki whispered. "What place is this?"

The unseen man chuckled horribly. "Prison."

"Yes," Ki said again. His hands went out in exploration. He discovered that he was in a hard iron bunk, with no pillow and no bedding of any kind.

"Hold on," the man said, "I got a match here." There was a scraping sound and the light flared up.

For a second it blinded Ki; then he was able to see his surroundings. The cell was small and windowless. The door was barred, and he knew there were cells on the other side of the unlit corridor, for he could just barely distinguish bars out there. He swung his gaze around to the man who was holding the match. It was burned down low, would flicker out in an instant. But that single instant was enough for Ki to see the other man's face. It was gaunt and emaciated, covered by a matted beard that might have been weeks old. The man was sitting on the bunk opposite, barely three feet away from Ki's.

The match burned out in the man's fingers, and the lone bit of light evaporated into the darkness. "These are the cells underneath the regular jail," the invisible man said. "This is where they put the secret prisoners. There's no record kept of men like us. We could rot here for the rest of our lives and no one would ever find us." The man stopped in a bout of raspy coughing. After a moment he spoke once more. "I don't think you're gonna be here long. When they brought you in I heard them say they'd come for you in a couple of hours."

"What's your name?" Ki asked. "If I get out of here, I'll see what I can do for you—"

He stopped because the other man had begun to laugh. It was harsh laughter that ended in more coughing. "Get out of here? F'get it. No one gets out of here except in a shroud. This is where the living dead are buried. Up above us is the jail where burglars, thieves, criminals of every description come in, serve their terms, and go out again. But for us down here there's no hope of that!"

"What do you mean?"

The other man's voice sounded like a far-off, Cassandra-like prophet of doom floating through the darkness. "There are fourteen or fifteen of us down here. Our only crimes were that we bucked Alderman Churlak and the administration. Nobody in Chicago has an inkling that these cells exist at all. When Churlak took power, he made this basement wing off limits, and he buries his enemies alive in here!"

Ki sat up quickly on his bunk, moving despite the throbbing of his injuries. The pain was forgotten in the sudden eagerness of his next question. "Listen, do you know if they've put Jessica Starbuck down here?"

"I don't know. I've only been here four months." He hesitated, hearing as Ki did the grating of a heavy door somewhere. Then the bobbing light of a lantern flickered far down the corridor, followed by the sound of heavy, measured steps. "The jailers!" he hissed. "They must be coming for you. I heard 'em say they'd be back to take you upstairs for a li'l session. They want to make you talk about something."

"A confession," Ki reckoned.

"Take a tip from me," the other man continued breathlessly, as if what he had to say had to be said now or never. "Give 'em what they want, fast. I've heard the moans of men who were brought back from those sessions. Sometimes they never come back. Believe me, it's better to talk."

The measured steps of the jailers stopped just outside their cell door. The lantern was raised high and flashed into the cell, blinding them. "This is it," a voice said. The cell door was opened. "Come with us, chink!"

Before Ki could comply, two jailers moved into the cell and seized him by the arms. They dragged him up from the bunk. A fiery, stabbing pain ripped through his arms and shoulders, but he said nothing. He brought his right knee up in a sudden blow to the groin of the jailer on the right, and the man howled with pain. The other guard smashed a nightstick across Ki's midriff, and Ki went crashing back into the bunk. He lay still, closing his eyes, trying to catch his breath.

"You knocked him out," the first jailer grunted. "C'mon, we gotta tote him."

Ki was seized roughly by the shoulders and legs and was half carried, half dragged out of the cell. The pains wracking his body became sharp and hot, but he let himself be hauled. And then, after the cell door had clanged shut and he was being lugged down the corridor, a terrible sound arose. It was the wild and frenzied shouting of the other hapless prisoners in those cells. How many there were was hard to guess. They bellowed and screamed, raising a dreadful clamor. The jailers cursed and hurried a bit; Ki was carried through a doorway, and the door clanged shut, closing out those horrid shouts.

Ki opened his eyes and said, "Okay, okay, I can walk."

The jailers let him down but kept a grip on his arms. One of them carried a lantern. They led him through a dank passage and up an almost interminable flight of stairs, then into a room that was ugly and bare except for two chairs and a table. But there was a single, small grilled window high up in the wall, and through that window Ki could see that it was nighttime outside.

The two chairs were occupied, one by Detective Brody and the other by another plainclothesman— brutish, hairy, so massive that when he stood up, Ki was surprised his knuckles didn't drag on the floor. Brody's face was twisted into a grin of ugly anticipation. "Get out," he said to the jailers. "When we're through with him, we'll knock on the door."

The jailers nodded, went out, and locked the door from the outside.

Brody rose from his chair and with mock solicitude said, "Won't you have a seat?" His cunning intention was written all over his features. If Ki went to sit down, he'd pull the chair away.

"Sit on it yourself," Ki said. "You look tired."

The other man was about to burst into an angry flood of invective, but Brody waved him to silence. "Look here, Ki, you're no fool. You know why we're here. You and Miz Starbuck are caught for murder, a hangin' offense here in Illinois like in Texas. But maybe we can cut a deal, if you're willin' to cooperate."

"I'm not making a case for you by confessing."

"Wise fucker!" The other cop stepped forward and drove a fist at Ki.

Moving his head a bit, Ki had no difficulty in evading the blow.

"Lay off, Lemmon!" Brody barked. "That'll come later."

Ki's eyes flickered with a sudden ray of hope. Lemmon looked like a powerful bruiser, perhaps one who had once been a professional fighter. Yet it had been a simple matter to duck that haymaker.

Brody was giving Ki a puzzled stare. "I don't get you at all, chink. We got you dead to rights. You shot Cyrene Yarbrough because she threatened to retract her statement that she'd spent the night with you. You could've easily risen in the middle of the night, gone over and plugged Emerson on orders from that Starbuck bitch, in reprisal for Emerson's shooting of Whitworth."

"Now, why would the brunette want to change her story?"

"She was jealous, that's why. You'd come to Chicago with Miss Starbuck, and it was hinted that you two were cuddly, and you went back to her after you—how'd they say in court?—had your way with the deceased dame."

Ki laughed. "Crap."

"Tell that to the jury." Brody smiled twistedly. "Yarbrough's cleaning lady, named Birdie as I rec'lect, saw you and Miz Starbuck hightailin' out the back door. Her identification was verified when we found where you'd parked your buggy, and the very manner in which you'd parked it—hiding it from view at a distance from her house—proves your intent. We gotcha, you bastard."

"You still got Mrs. Emerson?"

"Naw, she's been released. Her confession was made 'cause she thought her ol' man, the judge, had killed her husband. Not like your confession, which's gonna stick."

"And you know where you can stick it."

"Lemmon!" Brody snapped. "Let's change his fuckin' mind."

"My pleasure." Lemmon took out a small, wicked-looking sap with a leather thong attached to it. He smacked it down against the palm of his hand once with an ominous *thud*, as Brody reached in his back pocket and produced a set of brass knuckles, which he fitted onto his right hand.

Lemmon made the opening move, coming in swinging his sap. Ki sidestepped, avoiding the downward swipe, but in ducking the blackjack, he walked into a jab from Brody's brass knuckles, which gashed his left cheek. Brody's eyes were glittering. "I'll cut you up to chow mein, and after that I'll break your back!" He moved in again, jabbing with the brass knuckles. Ki came in under the jab and thrust his hand, palm forward, against Brody's chin. As he did so, he straightened his arm so that Brody's head was snapped back. At the same time Ki spread the fingers of his hand, making to gouge Brody's eyes. The move served two purposes—it threw Brody off balance and at the same time switched him from the offensive to the defensive, for it is instinctive to protect the eyes.

Brody reacted that way. He raised both hands to grab at Ki's one. Ki pushed his other hand hard into Brody's chest, shoving the already off-balance man backward. Brody clutched wildly, trying to regain his balance, and Ki thrust his hand under Brody's jacket, seized the butt of his service revolver, and yanked it out.

Lemmon had been coming in with his blackjack raised, and Ki swung around, thrust the revolver forward, and fired, all in one fluid motion. The revolver blasted deafeningly in the small room, and the slug bored through Lemmon's chest at such close range that it scorched his shirtfront. The sap hung limp by the thong from Lemmon's wrist as he threw his arms up in the air. The force of the bullet drove him backward, and he crashed into the table, carrying it with him down to the floor, where he lay with blood bubbling from his mouth.

Brody had recovered his balance. He stood transfixed, looking into the muzzle of the revolver, a baffled look on his face.

Out in the corridor, one of the jailers knocked at the door. "Hey, in there! Was that a shot we heard?"

Ki motioned to Brody with the revolver. "I want them in here."

"Go to hell!" Brody snarled.

Ki smiled. His finger curled tightly around the trigger.

"No, wait!" Brody exclaimed. He raised his voice, calling to the jailers. "It's all right! My gun went off by accident, but nobody was hurt. Come ahead in."

The lock clicked and the door was swung open. The two jailers entered and stopped short under the threat of Ki's revolver. They stared from the gun to the bloody dying figure of Lemmon on the floor.

Uttering swift commands that brooked no opposition, Ki lined Brody and the two jailers with their faces to the wall. He got handcuffs from Lemmon's and Brody's pockets and used them to cuff the three men's wrists together, running the links of one pair of cuffs around a steam pipe. He got a set of keys from one of the jailers, and two extra pistols, which he thrust into his waistband. Leaving the three manacled men and the dying man in the room, he snatched up the jailers' lantern, went out, and locked the door on the outside.

The corridor in which he found himself was a short one. It ended a few feet away in a staircase that led upward, probably to the prison proper. That way lay the path to freedom. But in the other direction—the way by which he had come with the jailers—there was a staircase that led down into the basement where he had been confined. Down there in the cells were men who rotted because they had dared challenge Alderman Churlak's power. And it was also possible that down there might be found Jessie.

Ki did not hesitate. He flashed the lantern in that direction and followed the staircase down to the door through which he had been carried. He tried the largest key on the massive padlock that held the iron bar across the sturdy oak door. The lock clicked open, and Ki had to put the lantern down on the floor while he removed the heavy iron bar. When he got the bar off, he took hold of the door handle, braced himself with his foot against the lintel, and pulled. Slowly the huge door creaked open. Picking up the lantern, he held it aloft, throwing the light into the cell block.

He shuddered at sight of the two rows of barred cells and the bearded, unkempt, dull-eyed faces of the prisoners who pressed close to the doors, wondering what visitation this was. As he moved down the corridor, the prisoners, seeing him, raised a shout of wonder. They had seen him carried out only a short while ago by the light of the lantern, and they had expected to see him brought back bruised, battered, and bleeding—or to never see him again. Instead they saw him returning, carrying the lantern himself and unaccompanied by the jailers.

Their shouts of wonder were changed to little whimpers of unbelieving joy as they saw him move from cell to cell, putting the lantern down and trying his keys on every cell door in the block until it was thrown wide open. Fourteen in all came crowding out into the corridor from their cells, thronging about Ki, their bodies showing white and sickly through the rents and tears of their tattered clothing, their beards long and uncut, some barely able to walk in the sudden release from the cramped cells. Some had festering sores, and others had open cuts where they had been struck by the jailers. The eyes of some were dull and beaten; the eyes of others were fierce and exultant in their new freedom.

And above it all was the constant clamor of their jabbering queries—demands to know how Ki had done it, who each of them was, what each man had done to land him here. *Bernard Crater, judge of the Criminal Court; I refused to dismiss a case against two of Churlak's enforcers . . . Samuel Grey, patrolman, first-grade; I made an arrest against Churlak's orders . . .* And so it went, from mouth to mouth, the roster of honorable men who had tried to resist the vicious machine of Alderman Churlak.

Ki listened impatiently, finally asking testily, "Do any of you know about Miss Jessica Starbuck? Do you know where she might be?"

There was a short moment of silence. Then an elderly man pushed forward; he had given the name of Arthur Preston, a former city accountant. "Not for sure, Ki, but I noticed the jailers goin' down to the far end of the cell block. I always thought it was a storeroom, but p'r'aps there are other cells there."

Ki's eyes glittered. He picked up the lantern and moved down the corridor, with the others crowding around. But then Ki stopped short, looking back toward the open door through which he had come. "I've taken care of the two jailers who dragged me out of here. But what if others come?"

There were gasps of surprise from the tattered men. In the sudden shock of what had just occurred they had forgotten that they were not yet free of their prison. "They inspect the cell block every day," one of them said. "A guard with a shotgun comes through. He may show up at any time."

Ki put down the lantern. Out of his pockets he took the three revolvers he had commandeered from Brody and the two jailers. He laid them on the floor, one by one. "Here're your weapons. Which of you are ready to put up a fight for your freedom?"

A dozen hands snatched at the guns. Three men got them, among them Patrolman Grey. The other two were men with raging, determined glints in their eyes. Patrolman Grey seemed to speak for them all when he declared, "I'd druther die fighting than rot to death down here!" He led the other two armed men out toward the stairs, followed by the others who were eager to fight even with bare hands.

And now Ki turned his attention to the door at the far end of the cell block. It, too, was a massive door with an iron bar padlocked across it. He had no lack of willing hands to remove the bar and to swing the heavy door wide open after he had opened the padlock. He held the lantern high, and the light revealed another stone staircase, thrusting itself far down into the lower bowels of the earth.

"I'm going down there," he said. "Don't forget, all of you, that you aren't free by a long shot. It won't be easy to fight your way out of this prison, and you may all die in the attempt."

"So much the better," Judge Crater said.

Nodding, Ki started down the dank stairs, hugging the wall with his right side, holding the lantern in his left hand. There were thirty-two steps. Ki counted them subconsciously. Thirty-two steps down until he stood at the bottom, feeling the throb of his muscles and bones. But his aches were as nothing to what those tattered fourteen men up above had endured. It seemed to him, when he had seen them in the lantern light, that nothing could be worse. Yet he dreaded to see what he might find down here.

He played the light around the space in which he found himself. It was a square chamber, hewn out of solid rock, perhaps at the pain and misery of a thousand convicts. In a wall opposite the stairs there was a small barred door, barely three feet high—just enough for a man to crawl through on hands and knees. Ki shuddered. He laid the lantern on the floor and heaved at the bar; there was no padlock here, merely the bar lying across two hasps. He got it off and let it clatter to the floor.

The ugly, fetid smell of old sweat and excrement leapt out at him from the black hole that the open door revealed. A voice spoke to him out of that ghastly tomb—a voice that rang defiantly: "If you figure dumping me in here will scare me into a confession, figure again! Why don't you come in here, you bastards? Come in with a gun or a knife, anything you want, and I'll scratch your eyes out!"

"Jessie!" Ki bent low and threw the beam of his lantern into the rocky cage. "C'mon out! You're free!"

"Ki? Glory to God!" Jessie exclaimed. A moment later she appeared in the opening, dirty, hair straggly, but smiling with relief. Hastily she crawled all the way out, her once fashionably smart outfit stained and smeared, beyond cleaning. Standing up, she hugged Ki thankfully, oblivious to what lay between them and freedom.

From up above there came the sound of a shotgun blast, and then two revolver shots. The sounds reverberated down the stairs and rolled against the walls. Then there was silence again.

Jessie looked inquiringly at Ki.

"The prisoners," Ki said, and swiftly explained the situation. "I released them and they must've ambushed the guard."

"Then there's a chance to get at Churlak?"

"If we get out of here alive. I'd sure like my weapons."

"Your clothes are up in a room next to the one where you were interrogated. That's where Brody took my bag away, too, after he found my derringer in it," Jessie said. She stooped and picked up the iron bar that had held the door. "I'll break a few heads with this!"

Together they made their way up the stairs.

In the cell block they found eleven of the fourteen prisoners alive. They had ambushed the guard coming down from above, and he had managed to get in one burst, killing three of them before he went down with a bullet in his brain. But now they had a shotgun and a satchel of shells.

"I think more of 'em are coming down," Patrolman Grey said. "They must've heard the shooting."

They moved up the stairs in a body, that wild and tattered array of desperate men and one woman, and in the upper hall they met the first of the prison guards, hurrying down to investigate the shooting. Those guards didn't stand a chance. They died without realizing just what was taking place, and their weapons increased the striking power of the small army of ghostly warriors who stormed the main jail block, capturing the guards there, then moved across the front yard, under a hail of carbine bullets from the two towers on the walls, and took the administration building.

In twenty minutes it was all over, and the seven survivors out of the original fourteen—plus Jessie and Ki—were in control of the jail. The prisoners in the regular cell blocks, thinking it was a general breakout, set up a howl to be released, but the survivors would have none of it.

"We'll not set those felons and murderers loose upon Chicago!" Judge Crater declared. "We're fighting for the right—and we'll fight the right way!"

"But how can we beat Vaughn Churlak and his political machine?" Ki demanded. "There're only seven of us, seven against a city!"

"I think I have a way," Jessie said quietly.

Chapter 11

Unlike Ichabod Temple's offices downtown, his house was unpretentious, a modest stone-and-wood cottage set in the middle of a corner lot that had probably cost more than the building itself. This was a nice, self-respecting middle-class community where folks went to bed reasonably early.

Temple's house showed no light at all. Jessie and Ki reined in their horses—police mounts they had borrowed from the jail stable—and walked to the porch, where Jessie twisted the doorbell. There was no answer. They tried knocking, but that didn't do any good either. Going around back, they found the door to a rear screened porch locked.

Ki was a little sick of locked doors. Asking for a handkerchief from Jessie, he wrapped it around his fist, put the fist smack through the wire screening, then reached through the hole and unlatched the door for them. They risked lighting a kerosene lamp they found inside and swiftly went through the entire house, until they were sure they were alone.

There were two bedrooms, one of them showing a woman's not-too-recent occupancy. Everything was neat, but there was a fine coating of dust on all of it and the smell of a room that had been closed up for some time. At the windows both the shades and drapes were drawn. The clothes in the closet were those of a woman well past the prime of life. Jessie and Ki decided she must be Ike Temple's sister, or maybe an aunt.

The second bedroom was clean but untidy, with the same untidiness Temple showed about his person. The bed looked as though Temple himself had made it, carelessly, with one hand, while putting on his pants. There was a small, carved kneehole desk with papers scattered over it that Jessie thought might be interesting, and she began a methodical search of its contents. She found nothing she considered relevant until, far at the back, she came upon a small packet of letters addressed to Temple in a woman's handwriting.

"Well, well," Jessie murmured, opening one and reading the signature first: *Opal*. Some of the others were signed just *O*, or *O.N.* There were no dates, but the ink was faded a little, as though the letters had been written a long time ago. "Look at these, Ki. Offhand, judging by the N, I'd say that Miss Opal Nichol's correspondence ceased when she married Lewis Emerson."

Quite unashamedly they read a few excerpts. There were no hot passages. Mostly the lady seemed to be fending Temple off, and in the last one she wrote kindly but definitely that she was marrying someone else. There was a postscript that almost stood Jessie on her ear, not because the news it conveyed was exactly unexpected, but because Temple and everyone else appeared to have forgotten it. She was tying the letters carefully together again when they heard a buggy enter the driveway on the other side of the house. Ki blew out the lamp, and they padded quietly to the parlor, where Jessie sat down on the divan and took out her derringer.

They were in no hurry now; in fact they were just waiting for Ichabod Temple to finish tending his buggy horse in the small barn adjoining the house. Presently feet scraped on the front porch, a key fumbled in the lock, and Temple walked in unsteadily, wavering a bit as he closed the door behind him. Ki relit the lamp then, and Temple, blinking in the sudden light, looked as if he'd run into an invisible wall. His eyes went with fright from Ki to Jessie to the derringer in Jessie's hand. Then he blurted, "What? What d'you want?"

"What you were looking for at Miss Yarbrough's."

"Where?"

"Would I be holding a gun on you if I didn't know you were there? We saw you. You ripped her place apart, came out, remembered your hat, and went back in again. With a key." Jessie stared at Temple's throat. Quite suddenly she saw that the man was drunk—not blind drunk, but drunk. She waved the gun at a chair. "You would be tight. Now, sit down before you fall down."

"No," Temple said.

"Sit!"

Temple seemed to fold in sections till his bottom rested on the chair. "I don't know what you want of me, but whatever it is, you can shoot and be damned." His body became rigid, bracing itself for the impact of the expected bullet.

Jessie leaned closer. "You kill her, Ike?"

Surprise, apparently genuine surprise, straightened Temple in the chair. "Me?" A bony hand pushed lank black hair out of his eyes. "You know better than that. You killed her." Sudden anger overcame his fear of the gun. "Yes, by God, and tried to nail your other murders on an innocent woman!"

Ki responded, menacingly: "You know we didn't, because she was dead when you left, and it was after that when the maid showed up and saw us." He made a gesture, as if threatening to hit Temple. "I don't like you much, chum. Just by opening your mouth you could have cleared us, but you didn't do it. You weren't going to do it."

Temple stared at Ki. "By God, I—" He sank back into the chair and buried his face in his hands. "All right, I was out there. I even forced myself to search the house afterward. But I didn't— I couldn't have—" The sudden rush of words clogged his throat. "My mother always wanted me to be a minister. I had to drink two quarts of liquor to get the picture of Cyrene out of my mind!"

Jessie asked, "What'd you find?"

"Nothing."

"What were you looking for?"

"I don't know. It was just that . . . well, there was a tie-up between her and Emerson, somewhere, and I felt I had to do something to help square him . . ." His voice dwindled away. "You want me to turn myself in, is that it? My neck for yours?"

Jessie lifted her gun. "You haven't much choice, have you?"

"I won't do it!"

"You won't like it, but you'll do it," Jessie said sharply. "And if you're lucky enough to be able to explain it without admitting you killed her, it may throw Opal Emerson right back in jail where she was. But so far you haven't said anything that proves you didn't kill her."

"Nor have you!"

Jessie appeared to think that over. "Tell you what we'll do," she said presently. "I know we didn't do it. And maybe you know you didn't." Her eyes were bright, watchful. "People who frame other people are always bound to be a little nervous, especially if they can't find the person they've framed. Now, you being there was as unforeseen as the maid showing up. As it

152

happened, the maid didn't hurt the framers any, but they don't know that you were there, too, that you can give us an iron-clad alibi. When they find out, when you tell them, what do you think is going to happen?"

Temple licked suddenly parched lips. "My God, I—"

Jessie nodded. "You'll be in a spot, all right, but you're in a spot anyway." She reached in her bag, brought out a small pad of telegram message blanks, and tossed it in Temple's lap. "We picked the pad up at the telegraph office on our way here. It's open all night, and will deliver messages anywhere in the city within an hour. Make up your mind, Ike. Like Ki says, we've taken quite a shellacking in Chicago, and we're all fed up!"

Temple asked for pen and ink.

Ki made the trip to the telegraph office and back.

And then they waited. This time managing to wait was harder. It wasn't only the physical discomfort of standing perfectly still in the narrow confines of the coat closet. Watching a nervous, unpredictable Ichabod Temple through a practically nonexistent crack between door and jamb was the worst. Temple kept moving about, and frequently Jessie and Ki would lose sight of him entirely. Considering that Temple was supposed to be a decoy, this was bad. Jessie felt like a hunter in a duck blind whose wooden birds had suddenly developed wings. Not that she blamed Temple for exhibiting nervousness. An unarmed man about to come face-to-face with a desperate murderer, and not knowing from which direction the attack would come, is not in the pleasantest spot in the world. Just the same, Jessie wished he would do his pacing in smaller circles.

As the minutes dragged by she wondered if perhaps she hadn't guessed wrong. Common sense told her that she must be right, but in spite of herself she felt a nagging suspicion that somewhere, somehow, she had slipped up. She was not as yet even sure of Ike Temple.

And then, quite suddenly, a man was standing there in the living room arch. There had been no sound to herald his approach, no telltale click of the door latch, no footfall on the carpet of the entryway. He was just there, facing into the room, his back to the coat closet. He, too, had a gun in his hand. He was Detective Brody.

Seeing him was a development Jessie had not anticipated. He and the two jailers Ki had handcuffed had been gone when the prisoners stormed the interrogation room, but finding him back on the attack so soon came as a surprise.

Temple was more than surprised; he was scared, and he had every right to be scared. "What's the— Put the gun down!"

Brody's laugh ran slyly around the corners of the room. "So you want to tell the police something, eh?" He took a slow step forward. He lifted his service revolver perhaps half an inch and then steadied it. "Tell 'em this—"

Jessie came out of the closet, Ki a step behind. "Brody!"

For a split instant no one moved. Then Brody lurched sideways, fell on one knee and one hand, swung and fired in one motion.

Ki launched into a *tobi-geri*, a flying snap-kick, aiming to strike the man's solar plexus but not to kill. Simultaneously with his spring, the bullet from Brody's gun whipped by his ear to bury itself in the closet door jamb. Before Brody could trigger again, Ki's extended left foot caught him in the upper chest, sending him backward into a credenza, the revolver sailing out of his hand as he smashed hard against the mahogany panels, splintering them into pieces. He went down flat amid the wreckage of wood and fine chinaware, slack-jawed and dazed, the wind knocked out of him.

Jessie looked at Temple. "Satisfied?"

Temple gulped. "Yes, I—" His eyes were suddenly more frightened than Brody's. "Of course, I'm satisfied."

Jessie stared at Brody as he lay gasping on the floor. "There's nothing crookeder than a crooked cop, I guess. The trouble with guys like you is that you never learn there's always another guy behind the one in front of you. The law of averages gets you."

"G-guess you're right," Brody panted in a voice drained of all emotion. He tried to rise, fell back again. His next move must have been planned very carefully, for he actually had a second gun out of his hip pocket and pointed before Jessie realized that the attempt to rise had been faked.

Ike Temple startled them all. As though imitating Ki, he lashed out with one of his long legs in a terrific kick, missing the gun entirely and connecting with the side of Brody's head. There was the sharply brittle sound of a snapping stick. Brody collapsed like a deflated sack.

Jessie plunged down and seized Brody's head in her two hands. She turned it back and forth. The neck offered no more resistance than a piece of rope. Eyes in which there was no longer any life mocked her. She turned a face white with fury on Ike Temple. "You've broken his neck!"

Temple looked at her stupidly. "Is it so important?" He retched a little. "I mean, well, after all, I saved your life, you know."

Jessie didn't seem particularly grateful. "And a fat lot of good it's going to do me. We finally get someone in a spot where we can make him talk and what happens? He has to go and get his head kicked off." She sat back on her haunches, listening. Apparently either everybody in the neighborhood was stone deaf, or the drapes at the windows had muffled the shot. She eyed Temple narrowly. "I wonder if you didn't—"

Temple sucked in his breath. "You know better than that!"

"Do I?" They glared at each other for a long moment. Then, sighing, Jessie turned to Ki. "Well, maybe. For certain we've now got to pull another bluff. I'm afraid this is turning into a long night . . ."

An hour and a half later, Jessie had arranged it so that two men were facing each other across a broad polished desk. The room was big but had a warm, comfortable feel, with books that looked as though they might have been read lining one whole wall except for the fireplace. There was a newly-lit fire in the hearth, and beside it an open Gladstone bag lay on its side, spewing papers out on the carpet.

In many ways the two men were alike. Each was well on toward middle age. Both wore dinner jackets, though Ruben Garibaldi's leaning toward cummerbunds instead of vests gave him a certain flair that in some circles was known as flash. His dark, heavy, almost sullen expression, however, contrasted with Thurlow Dobbs's ruddy-cheeked, smiling features.

Out on the flagged terrace beyond closed French doors, Jessie and Ki watched both of them and trusted neither. It was true that Garibaldi was there at Jessie's instigation, but it was a little early yet to reckon how far, or in what direction, the crime boss would go. Their voices filtered out, only a little muffled by the glass doors.

Garibaldi was saying, "So you weren't going to let me know."

Dobbs leaned forward in his desk chair. His smile was gone. "I was, Ruben. I swear I was. In fact I left word for you to contact me the minute you came in."

"No," Garibaldi said. He neither moved nor lifted his voice. "I've been right behind you, or one of my sons has, ever since you got a certain telegram."

Dobbs was smiling again. "Very well, then I didn't." His eyes were clear, guileless. "Prove I didn't intend to."

"In my set," Garibaldi said stonily, "you don't always wait for proof." A gesture indicated the Gladstone. "You gutted your private boxes down at the bank. I want to do the same thing. Now."

Dobbs's chair creaked. "Well, about that, Ruben, I don't know. The keys—"

"You've got duplicates."

"To mine, maybe."

"To all of 'em." Garibaldi held out a hand. "Give."

Dobbs stood up violently. "I tell you I haven't got them. You'll have to wait till morning."

Garibaldi nodded, as though communing with himself. "So that's it. You dumped enough stuff in my safe deposit box to hang the whole business on me. Jessica Starbuck said you would. She said—"

"Starbuck!" Thurlow Dobbs's belly shook with laughter. "Don't tell me you'd take the word of that spoiled young vixen against mine."

"She's been right on the mark so far." Again Garibaldi looked at the well-filled Gladstone. "Let's go back down to the bank and prove she's wrong about this."

"No." Dobbs leaned forward, balanced on the balls of his feet. "Aren't you forgetting something, Ruben? Aren't you forgetting who asks the questions around here?"

"That was yesterday," Garibaldi said. "Today, tonight, now, it's Garibaldi asking the questions." His voice thickened. "And getting the wrong answers." He put a large right hand flat against the cummerbund about his middle. Then there was a pistol in the hand. "Look at it, *Mister* Dobbs."

157

Out on the terrace Jessie nodded to Ki. Ki put a foot against the jointure of the French doors; the catch snapped with a sound little louder than Brody's neck had made. They entered swiftly, Jessie saying, "Don't make me shoot." Light from a desk lamp glinted on the barrel of Brody's service revolver.

Garibaldi didn't turn, didn't take his eyes off Thurlow Dobbs. "I kind of liked the brunette, *Mister* Dobbs. You did her in."

Dobbs's face had lost a little of its color, but there was no sign of fear in his eyes. "Jessica Starbuck tell you that, too?"

"I told him you had it done," Jessie responded. "Brody was no more responsible than a gun is responsible if someone points it and squeezes the trigger."

"Brody?"

"Yes," Jessie said. "You see, we've got Brody. We've had him ever since you made the mistake of sending him after Ichabod Temple." She looked sideways at Garibaldi. "Keep out of this. He's mine." She looked back at Dobbs. "If that's a gun you're reaching for in the drawer, you'd better—"

"A gun?" Dobbs appeared surprised. "No, I'd hardly try matching shots with a hysterical lady and a gentleman as experienced as Ruben here. I was merely thinking of ringing for my man, to have you shown out." He laughed in gentle derision. "You see, even had I done all the things you accuse me of doing, Miss Starbuck, neither Brody nor Ruben is exactly in a position to testify against me. On the practical side"—he paused and looked intently at Garibaldi—"some safe deposit keys would fix you up pretty nicely, Ruben. If you were to turn that gun on Miss Starbuck and her henchman, I assure you—"

Fear crawled up Jessie's spine; she forced herself to relax. "You don't seem to understand about this. Any of it." From the tail of her eye she watched the motionless Garibaldi. "Anything a man like Ruben Garibaldi hates, it's to be made a sucker of. He knows you've made a sucker of him and that you'll do it again if you get the chance." She drew a slow breath. "So there isn't any question of taking you into court."

"Well, let's pretend this is it," Dobbs said equably. "Why don't you shoot her, Ruben, both of them? You can, you know, and be praised by all the forces of law and order. They're wanted criminals. It's a simple little thing to do in return for the keys to evidence which might incriminate you."

"There're two of us against you," Jessie argued. "Also, if a Garibaldi has had you tailed ever since you left to go to the bank, he knows you must have the keys on you." She saw that her logic had registered on Garibaldi.

Dobbs saw it, too. "So it's down to deciding who's to be my executioner, is that it?" He decided that for himself. He fell forward out of his chair behind the desk; a drawer slid open; there was a single muffled shot. When Jessie, Ki, and Garibaldi got around to looking at him, they saw that he had put the gun in his mouth. There was no longer any back of his head.

"I'm sorry," Garibaldi said to Jessie, straightening. There was that peeping sound again as he blew on his silver whistle. In from the terrace rushed his four sons, revolvers in hand; they spread out like points on a compass, covering Jessie and Ki. Ruben Garibaldi drew his lips back over his teeth in a malevolent grin. "I'm really sorry, Miss Starbuck. I guess you think I'm double-crossing you, and maybe I am, but believe me, I wish there was another way. But I can't afford to leave no witnesses, you understand."

Those were the last words Ruben Garibaldi ever spoke on earth. A slim throwing dagger pierced his spine between his kidneys, and he twisted and pitched forward, screaming horribly in the remaining seconds of his life.

Ki stood by the desk, his hands dealing daggers and *shuriken* in almost one continuous stream, with split-second intervals between throws. He felt the heavy-caliber slugs whining past his head as the Garibaldi sons opened quick but ill-aimed fire. One or two shots splintered the desk. He was aiming at Ben and Al, and he saw Ben's lantern jaw with its dirty yellow stubble go slack and bloody as his head rolled on his limp neck and lobbed forward, pulling him down. Then Al's revolver slid from his hand, and he clawed at his guts with both big, dirty hands. His knees buckled, and he tipped over as he fell.

Siding Ki, Jessie kept thumbing back the hammer and pulling the trigger of Brody's pistol, adding to the crashing echoes of gunfire. She saw Pete Garibaldi's head jerk crazily, and then it came down as if he were ducking something, and the front of his forehead above the bridge of his hawk nose was a gaping hope filled with spurting blood. As Pete piled up in a shapeless heap, a *shuriken* slashed into Nate Garibaldi between the shoulders. Another razor-edged disk hit him lower as he stiffened, and bent him backward. He was dead when he hit the floor.

Through the haze of gunpowder smoke that layered the lamplight, Ki saw Jessie standing there with Brody's gun in hand. He smiled thinly at her, but his eyes were bleak as he stepped across the dead body of Ruben Garibaldi, who was no longer screaming. His screams had died with the last reverberating gun echoes.

Chapter 12

Judge Marvin Nichol's library looked crowded, cluttered. From over the ornate mantel a fine-looking old gentleman in white stock and ruffles peered out of a heavy gold frame in aristocratic disapproval of the judge's somewhat ill-assorted visitors. Jessie tended to agree with the portrait. She watched Ichabod Temple and Judge Nichol glaring at each other. Chief of Police Felix Weims was there, but he wasn't doing much glaring. Alderman Vaughn Churlak was conspicuous by his absence.

Judge Nichol fixed Weims with an irate eye. "Am I to understand that all"—he waved at Thurlow Dobbs's Gladstone bag—"all this has been going on without your knowledge?"

Weims's face became a deeper red. "You didn't find nothing in there about me, did you?"

"Then all I've got to say is you're a blithering dope!"

"Okay, I'm a dope." The chief regarded the unfriendly faces about him. "P'r'aps I heard talk, but talk ain't proof. The rest of you heard the same kind of stuff I did. Did you get anywhere with it?"

"And maybe you were told to close your ears against what you did hear!"

"If you hope to hang anything on me through my support of Alderman Churlak, you can go fu— hang yourself!"

Jessie could admire loyalty even in a fool like Weims. "Thurlow Dobbs didn't need the chief here," she said, "unless it was to take the rap if something went sour. He already had a third of the police department through Brody."

"That shit!" Weims said. Conscious of a lady present, he apologized to Jessie. "Sorry."

Judge Nichol cleared his throat. "Then it's your contention, Miss Starbuck, that Dobbs's inner circle consisted of Brody, Alderman Churlak, Cyrene Yarbrough, and Ruben Garibaldi?"

"Yes, and he was juggling even them," Jessie said, then qualified that. "At least Garibaldi, Churlak, and Cyrene. Brody was the liaison between them, but each of them didn't know about the business arrangement between Dobbs and the others."

"How can you be sure of that?"

"Because I used what I knew about Cyrene when I made a deal with Garibaldi. I showed him where Dobbs had been holding out on him, and that made him sore enough to play along with me—at least until he could double-cross me. It stands to reason if Dobbs was holding out on Garibaldi, he was holding out on the others."

Judge Nichol gnawed his lower lip. "I don't like it, this making deals with gangsters."

"What would you have done," Jessie retorted, "gone to the police? With what I've seen of the local gendarmes?"

Weims bridled. "Damn it, Miss Starbuck! Er, sorry, Miss Starbuck."

"Let's run through it all again," Ike Temple said, frowning, perplexed. "Thurlow Dobbs, in his capacity as Chicago's leading banker, was in a position to know who had money. So he conceived of a way of relieving them of it—two ways, if we are to believe the evidence. He arranged for Ruben Garibaldi and his family to handle the gambling, robberies, and other ordinary rackets, promising him police protection through Brody. The other angle was the brunette, who was to take care of those suckers who wouldn't knuckle under to threats, or those politicians and officials who weren't susceptible to bribes. She was the lure, the seductress who'd get the blackmail goods on her victims by . . ." He glanced uncomfortably at Jessie.

"I'm of age," Jessie said. "Don't mind me." She sighed a trifle enviously as she looked at the well-filled Gladstone. "There's close to half a million dollars in currency in there that shows Dobbs and the brunette did collect. How they did it isn't my concern. What is, is the motive behind all these recent killings." She turned to Nichol. "I'm afraid that's going to be a pretty delicate subject. Maybe the judge—"

"Miss Starbuck, you don't like me very well, do you?"

"I can't admit I do." Jessie paused, thinking about that for a moment. "Actually, this whole nasty affair stems from liking—or rather, loving. Judge Nichol loves his daughter and she loves him, and both of them are so stiff-necked with pride in themselves and the Nichol line that they couldn't give anyone else credit for a love bigger than theirs." She stood up and began moving about the room. "I'm talking about Lewis Emerson now. He took it on the chin—the insinuations that he was crooked; that he was neglecting his wife and spending his money on another woman—because he didn't want his wife to know her father was a heel, or a fool, or worse." She stared insolently at the judge.

"You just heard Ike Temple outline a blackmail scheme by Cyrene. Why didn't you tell us that it had happened to you?"

Judge Nichol flinched as though he had been struck. Then, proving that blood could be good for something, he ironed his face out and said steadily, "Because I didn't know it. It never occurred to me until just this moment that the incident—it was no more than that, so far as I knew—could have any bearing. No one ever approached me with anything to sell."

"No, Cyrene supplied proof—silly letters or receipts for expensive gifts—which Dobbs sold to Emerson. Dobbs picked him to bleed rather than you, because he knew Emerson would keep quiet, and it was his object to put the district attorney in as bad a light as possible."

Ike Temple scratched his hair. "Why?"

Jessie wondered if she should confess reading Temple's private mail. She decided she wouldn't if she didn't have to. "In his own peculiar way, Thurlow Dobbs loved Opal Nichol. When she became Opal Emerson it—well, it kind of soured him on the honest life and he became obsessed with the lust for power. Power and money. He still wanted Opal, though, but he knew he couldn't have her without getting rid of Emerson. And just having Emerson murdered wouldn't do any good. He had to make him look like a stinker to boot." She paused to look down at Temple, who was moodily cracking his bony knuckles. "I built up a pretty good case against you, too, Ike, on the same general theory. That was before I discovered that Dobbs had also been a suitor for Opal's hand. I figured a man in the real estate business had as good a chance to learn who was wealthy as a banker. Or say the head of a leading law firm." She did not look at Judge Nichol now. "This making sense to any of you?"

"Indeed so," Nichol allowed. "But why'd you narrow yourself down to just us as suspects?"

"Only you three on the council knew what Harold Whitworth was up to." Some of her earlier anger, and the bitterness, returned to her. "It didn't all come as easy as it sounds, you understand. For a while I thought Millicent had killed Emerson. And there were complicating factors. But when I began to pick on Opal Emerson, right away there was dutch to pay. Nobody wanted her annoyed, not even if I had to be gotten rid of, too. Obviously someone that loved her, you see. Her father loved her, naturally, and presently I guessed that Ike did, too. About Thurlow Dobbs I didn't know until tonight, but I still had him on the original count of being in on getting Harold Whitworth involved."

Ike Temple uttered something that sounded very much like a naughty word. "So you stirred up everybody to see what we'd all do."

"What else could I do?" Jessie countered. "The whole city dummied up on me. Nobody but a banker or a lawyer or a real estate operator could've thought up anything as complicated as it got after that. There were already three dead people—Harold Whitworth, Emerson, and probably Millicent Whitworth. And all to get one man: Emerson. After Millicent, I vowed to become a nuisance, so Pocker and Leo Hackette were hired along with Marie to take care of me. With me gone, no doubt Ki would've been next. Instead, that didn't work, and I raised such a squawk that Leo and Marie had to be killed. Brody saw to that, with the unconscious assistance of his chief."

Weims swore again, apologized again.

Jessie ignored him, continuing: "Then there was the Emerson inquest, when I caused Mrs. Emerson's arrest. That meant Cyrene Yarbrough would have to retract her story for Ki and leave him without an alibi."

Temple growled, "She didn't have to be killed."

"No," Jessie agreed. "That was more or less the giveaway. She could have reneged on Ki's alibi, but she didn't. So she was killed for another reason."

"I sort of needled her into checking up on her boss," Ki said, his smile holding no pleasure at the memory. "She found out what we hadn't, that Dobbs was in love with someone else and that she was never going to be a respected banker's wife. She probably raised hell about it. So she had to be killed before she spilled to us. So while they were doing it, they thought why not frame us for it, and when we're where we can't talk back, they'd stick us for all the rest, too." Ki scowled at Weims. "Brody put Jessie's gun in her bureau drawer right under your nose. It was so raw it stank. But did you see it? No, you were so dumb you stood there and let Brody try to jockey me into getting myself shot."

"Whaddyuh mean, dumb? I was prayin' you would!" Weims retorted angrily, then eyed Jessie. "Wait a minute. I can see how Dobbs had to send Brody after Ike Temple. You simply had Temple send him a message saying he knew for a fact you didn't kill the brunette. I don't see how you could be sure Dobbs was the one to notify."

"I wasn't sure," Jessie said. "I just thought he might be. This afternoon Cyrene remarked to Ki that I was 'lighting fires to see what boils,' which is very close to what I'd told Dobbs earlier. It's a rather unusual phrase. Of course, that's not much to go on, but while we were waiting for Ike Temple to come home, we ran across Dobbs's name again. Seems Opal wanted to make a rejected suitor feel better about being bounced, so she appended the information that she was giving one of his rivals the gate, too."

Temple choked, spluttering.

Judge Nichol passed a blue-veined hand over a face

that had aged ten years in the last ten minutes. "I'm not arguing with anyone. I just wonder why Thurlow should have come in with us, with the Civic Reform Council. His money helped elect Lewis, helped..." A little sob shook him as he said his son-in-law's name. "God, that I should've let myself be..."

Temple got up and put a hand on his shoulder. "I was partially responsible for that, Marvin. We'll... we'll see what we can do toward making him a hero for someone to remember."

For once Chief Weims showed wisdom. "Let's get out of here," he advised Jessie and Ki. "We can finish up at my office, about all this and the jail situation, too."

They left the two men standing there, a curiously pathetic ex-jurist and the realtor whose mother had wanted him to be a minister. Outside, breathing deep of the cool night air, Jessie said, "I'm not going to your office, Chief. You've got all there is."

Weims blew out his breath. "What I've got is trouble. I wish I was in Africa. The morning paper..." He looked at Jessie and Ki. "Is it going to buy you anything for everybody to know how dumb I am?"

"I don't care what happens to you," Jessie said frigidly. "I only wish I could be around to see you thrown out on your backside."

"Then you're leaving Chicago tonight?" Weims sounded hopeful.

"Just as soon as I can buy us train tickets," Jessie said fervently. She took Ki's arm. "Come on, let's go find out how soon that is."

Watch for

LONE STAR AND THE BRUTUS GANG

127th in the exciting LONE STAR series
from Jove

Coming in March!

SPECIAL PREVIEW

Giles Tippette, America's new star of the classic western, brings to life the adventures of an outlaw gone straight—who's got everything at stake facing a no-account gambler . . .

Dead Man's Poker

By the acclaimed author of *Gunpoint*, *Sixkiller*, and *Hard Rock*.

Here is a special excerpt from this authentic new western—available from Jove Books . . .

I was hurt, though how badly I didn't know. Some three hours earlier I'd been shot, the ball taking me in the left side of the chest about midway up my rib cage. I didn't know if the slug had broken a rib or just passed between two of them as it exited my back. I'd been in Galveston, trying to collect a gambling debt, when, like a fool kid, I'd walked into a setup that I'd ordinarily have seen coming from the top of a tree stump. I was angry that I hadn't collected the debt, I was more than angry that I'd been shot, but I was furious at myself for having been suckered in such a fashion. I figured if it ever got around that Wilson Young had been gotten that easy, all of the old enemies I'd made through the years would start coming out of the woodwork to pick over the carcass.

But, in a way, I was lucky. By rights I should have been killed outright, facing three of them as I had and having nothing to put me on the alert. They'd had guns in their hands by the time I realized it wasn't money I was going to get, but lead.

Now I was rattling along on a train an hour out of Galveston, headed for San Antonio. It had been lucky, me catching that train just as it was pulling out. Except for that, there was an excellent chance that I would have been incarcerated in Galveston and looking at more trouble than I'd been in in a long time. After the shooting I'd managed to get away from the office where the trouble had happened and make my way toward the depot. I'd been wearing a frock coat of a good quality linen when I'd sat down with Phil Sharp to discuss the money he owed me. Because it was a hot day, I took the coat off and laid it over the arm of the chair I was sitting in. When the shooting was over, I grabbed the coat and the little valise I was carrying and ducked and dodged my way through alleyways and side streets. I came up from the border on the train so, of course, I didn't have a horse with me.

But I did have a change of clothes, having expected to be overnight in Galveston. In an alley I took off my bloody shirt, inspected the wound in my chest, and then wrapped the shirt around me, hoping to keep the blood from showing. Then I put on a clean shirt that fortunately was dark and not white like the one I'd been shot in. After that I donned my frock coat, picked up my valise, and made my way to the train station. I did not know if the law was looking for me or not, but I waited until the train was ready to pull out before I boarded it. I had a round-trip ticket so there'd been no need for me to go inside the depot.

I knew I was bleeding, but I didn't know how long it would be before the blood seeped through my makeshift bandage and then through my shirt and finally showed on my coat.

All I knew was that I was hurting and hurting bad and that I was losing blood to the point where I was beginning to feel faint. It was a six-hour ride to San Antonio, and I was not at all sure I could last that long. Even if the blood didn't seep through enough to call it to someone's attention, I might well pass out.

But I didn't have many options. There were few stops between Galveston and San Antonio, it being a kind of a spur line, and what there were would be small towns that most likely wouldn't even have a doctor. I could get off in one and lay up in a hotel until I got better, but that didn't much appeal to me. I wanted to know how bad I was hurt, and the only way I was going to know that was to hang on until I could get to some good medical attention in San Antone.

I was Wilson Young, and in that year of 1896, I was thirty-two years old. For fourteen of those years, beginning when I was not quite fifteen, I had been a robber. I'd robbed banks, I'd robbed money shipments, I'd robbed high-stakes poker games, I'd robbed rich people carrying more cash than they ought to have been, but mostly I'd robbed banks. But then about four years past, I'd left the owlhoot trail and set out to become a citizen that did not constantly have to be on the lookout for the law. Through the years I'd lost a lot of friends and a lot of members of what the newspapers had chosen to call my "gang"—the Texas Bank Robbing Gang in one headline.

I'd even lost a wife, a woman I'd taken out of a whorehouse in the very same town I was now fleeing from. But Marianne hadn't been a whore at heart; she'd just been kind of briefly and unwillingly forced into it in much the same way I'd taken up robbing banks.

I had been making progress in my attempt to achieve a certain amount of respectability. At first I'd set up on the Mexican side of the border, making occasional forays into Texas to sort of test the waters. Then, as a few years passed and certain amounts of money found their way into the proper hands, I was slowly able to make my way around Texas. I had not been given a pardon by the governor, but emissaries of his had indicated that the state of Texas was happy to have no further trouble with Wilson Young and that the past could be forgotten so long as I did nothing to revive it.

And now had come this trouble. The right or wrong of my position would have nothing to do with it. I was still Wilson Young, and if I was in a place where guns were firing and men were being shot, the prevailing attitude was going to be that it was my doing.

So it wasn't only the wound that was troubling me greatly; it was also the worry about the aftermath of what had begun as a peaceful and lawful business trip. If I didn't die from my wound, there was every chance that I would become a wanted man again, and there would go the new life I had built for myself. And not only that life of peace and legality, but also a great deal of money that I had put into a business in Del Rio, Texas, right along the banks of the Rio Grande. Down there, a stone's throw from Mexico, I owned the most high-class saloon and gambling emporium and whorehouse as there was to be found in Texas. I had at first thought to put it on the Mexican side of the river, but the *mordida*, the bribes, that the officials would have taken convinced me to build it in Texas, where the local law was not quite so greedy. But now, if trouble were to come from this shooting, I'd have to be in Mexico, and my business would be in Texas. It might have been only a stone's throw away, but for me, it might just as well have been a thousand miles. And I'd sunk damn near every cent I had in the place.

My side was beginning to hurt worse with every mile. I supposed it was my wound, but the train was rattling around and swaying back and forth like it was running on crooked rails. I was in the last car before the caboose, and every time we rounded a curve, the car would rock back and forth like it was fixing to quit the tracks and take off across the prairie. Fortunately, the train wasn't very crowded and I had a seat to myself. I was sort of sitting in the middle of the double cushion and leaning to my right against the wall of the car. It seemed to make my side rest easier to stretch it out like that. My valise was at my feet, and with a little effort, I bent down and fumbled it open with my right hand. Since my wound had begun to stiffen up, my left arm had become practically useless—to use it would almost put tears in my eyes.

I had a bottle of whiskey in my valise, and I fumbled it out, pulled the cork with my teeth and then had a hard pull. There was a spinsterish middle-aged lady sitting right across the aisle from me, and she give me such a look of disapproval that I thought for a second that she was going to call the conductor and make a commotion. As best I could, I got the cork back in the bottle and then hid it out of sight between my right side and the wall of the car.

Outside, the terrain was rolling past. It was the coastal prairie of south Texas, acres and acres of flat, rolling plains that grew the best grazing grass in the state. It would stay that way until the train switched tracks and turned west for San Antonio. But that was another two hours away. My plan was to get myself fixed up in San Antone and then head out for Del Rio and the Mexican side of the border just as fast as I could. From there I'd try and find out just what sort of trouble I was in.

That was, if I lived that long.

With my right hand I pulled back the left side of my coat, lifting it gently, and looked underneath. I could see just the beginning of a stain on the dark blue shirt I'd changed into. Soon it would soak through my coat and someone would notice it. I had a handkerchief in my pocket, and I got that out and slipped it inside my shirt, just under the stain. I had no way of holding it there, but so long as I kept still, it would stay in place.

Of course I didn't know what was happening at my back. For all I knew the blood had already seeped through and stained my coat. That was all right so long as my back was against the seat, but it would be obvious as soon as I got up. I just had to hope there would be no interested people once I got to San Antone and tried to find a doctor.

I knew the bullet had come out my back. I knew it because I'd felt around and located the exit hole while I'd been hiding in the alley, using one shirt for a bandage and the other for a sop. Of course the hole in my back was bigger than the entrance hole the bullet had made. It was always that way, especially if a bullet hit something hard like a bone and went to tumbling or flattened out. I could have stuck my thumb in the hole in my back.

About the only good thing I could find to feel hopeful about was the angle of the shot. The bullet had gone in very near the bottom of my ribs and about six inches from my left side. But it had come out about only three or four inches from my side. That meant there was a pretty good chance that it had missed most of the vital stuff and such that a body has got inside itself. I knew it hadn't nicked my lungs because I was breathing fine. But there is a whole bunch of other stuff inside a man that a bullet ain't going to do a bit of good. I figured it had cracked a rib for sure because it hurt to breathe deep, but that didn't even necessarily have to be so. It was hurting so bad anyway that I near about couldn't separate the different kinds of hurt.

A more unlikely man than Phil Sharp to give me my seventh gunshot wound I could not have imagined. I had ended my career on the owlhoot trail with my body having lived through six gunshots. That, as far as I was concerned, had been a-plenty. By rights I should have been dead, and there had been times when I had been given up for dead. But once off the outlaw path I'd thought my days of having my blood spilt were over. Six was enough.

And then Phil Sharp had given me my seventh. As a gambler I didn't like the number. There was nothing lucky about it that I could see, and I figured that anything that wasn't lucky had to be unlucky.

Part of my bad luck was because I *was* Wilson Young. Even though I'd been retired for several years, I was still, strictly speaking, a wanted man. And if anybody had cause to take interest in my condition, it might mean law—and law would mean trouble.

For that matter Phil Sharp and the three men he'd had with him might have thought they could shoot me without fear of a murder charge because of the very fact of my past and my uncertain position with regard to the law, both local and through the state. Hell, for all I knew some of those rewards that had been posted on my head might still be lying around waiting for someone to claim them. It hadn't been so many years past that my name and my likeness had been on Wanted posters in every sheriff's office in every county in Texas.

I had gone to see Phil Sharp because he'd left my gambling house owing me better than twenty thousand dollars. I didn't, as an ordinary matter, advance credit at the gaming tables, but Sharp had been a good customer in the past and I knew him to be a well-to-do man. He owned a string of warehouses along the docks in Galveston, which was the biggest port in Texas. The debt had been about a month old when I decided to go and see him. When he'd left Del Rio, he'd promised to wire me the money as soon as he was home, but it had never come. Letters and telegrams jogging his memory had done no good, so I'd decided to call on him in person. It wasn't just the twenty thousand; there was also the matter that it ain't good policy for a man running a casino and cathouse to let word get around that he's careless about money owed him. And in that respect I was still the Wilson Young it was best not to get too chancy with. Sharp knew my reputation and I did not figure to have any trouble with him. If he didn't have the twenty thousand handy, I figured we could come to some sort of agreement as to how he could pay it off. I had wired him before I left Del Rio that I was planning a trip to Houston and was going to look in on him in Galveston. He'd wired back that he'd be expecting me.

I saw him in his office in the front of one of the warehouses he owned down along the waterfront. He was behind his desk when I was shown in, getting up to shake hands with me. He was dressed like he usually was, in an expensive suit with a shiny vest and a big silk tie. Sharp himself was a little round man in his forties with a kind of baby face and a look that promised you could trust him with your virgin sister. Except I'd seen him without the suit and vest, chasing one of my girls down the hall at four o'clock in the morning with a bottle of whiskey in one hand and the handle to his hoe in the other. I'd also seen him at the poker table with sweat pouring off his face as he tried to make a straight beat a full house. It hadn't then and it probably never would.

He acted all surprised that I hadn't gotten my money, claiming he'd mailed it to me no less than a week ago. He said, "I got to apologize for the delay, but I had to use most of my ready cash on some shipments to England. Just let me step in the next room and look at my canceled checks. I'd almost swear I saw it just the other day. Endorsed by you."

Like I said, he looked like a man that might shoot you full of holes in a business deal, but not the sort of man who could use or would use a gun.

He got up from his desk and went to a door at the back, just to my right. I took off my coat and laid it over the arm of the chair, it being warm in the office. I was sitting kind of forward on the chair, feeling a little uneasy for some reason. It was that, but it was mainly the way Sharp opened the back door that probably saved my life. When you're going through a door, you pull it to you and step to your left, toward the opening, so as to pass through. But Sharp pulled open the door and then stepped back. In that instant, I slid out of the chair I was sitting in and down to my knees. As I did, three men with hoods pulled over their heads came through the door with pistols in their hands. Their first volley would have killed me if I'd still been sitting in the chair. But they fired at where I'd been, and by the time they could cock their pistols for another round, I had my revolver in my hand and was firing. They never got off another shot; all three went down under my rapid-fire volley.

Then I became aware that Phil Sharp was still in the room, just by the open door. I was about to swing my revolver around on him when I saw a little gun in his hand. He fired, once, and hit me in the chest. I knew it was a low-caliber gun because the blow of the slug just twitched at my side, not even knocking me off balance.

But it surprised me so that it gave Sharp time to cut through the open door and disappear into the blackness of the warehouse. I fired one shot after him, knowing it was in vain, and then pulled the trigger on an empty chamber.

I had not brought any extra cartridges with me. In the second I stood there with an empty gun, I couldn't remember why I hadn't brought any extras, but the fact was that I was standing there, wounded, with what amounted to a useless piece of iron in my fist. As quick as I could, expecting people to suddenly come bursting in the door, I got over to where the three men were laying on the floor and began to check their pistols to see if they fired the same caliber ammunition I did. But I was out of luck. My revolver took a .40-caliber shell; all three of the hooded men were carrying .44-caliber pistols.

Two of the men were dead, but one of them was still alive. I didn't have time to mess with him, but I turned him over so he could hear me good and said, "Tell Phil Sharp I ain't through with him. Nor your bunch either."

Then I got out of there and started making my way for the train depot. At first the wound bothered me hardly at all. In fact at first I thought I'd just been grazed. But then, once outside, I saw the blood spreading all over the front of my shirt and I knew that I was indeed hit. I figured I'd been shot by nothing heavier than a .32-caliber revolver but a .32 can kill you just as quick as a cannon if it hits you in the right place.

From the Creators of Longarm!

LONE ★ STAR

Featuring the beautiful Jessica Starbuck and her loyal half-American half-Japanese martial arts sidekick Ki.

_LONE STAR AND THE TRAIL TO ABILENE #114	0-515-10791-3/$3.50
_LONE STAR AND THE HORSE THIEVES #115	0-515-10809-X/$3.50
_LONE STAR AND THE DEEPWATER PIRATES #116	0-515-10833-2/$3.50
_LONE STAR AND THE BLACK BANDANA GANG #117	0-515-10850-2/$3.50
_LONE STAR IN THE TIMBERLANDS #118	0-515-10866-9/$3.50
_LONE STAR AND THE MEXICAN MUSKETS #119	0-515-10881-2/$3.50
_LONE STAR AND THE SANTA FE SHOWDOWN #120	0-515-10902-9/$3.99
_LONE STAR AND THE GUNRUNNERS #121	0-515-10930-4/$3.99
_LONE STAR AND THE BUCCANEERS #122	0-515-10956-8/$3.99
_LONE STAR AND THE AZTEC TREASURE #123	0-515-10981-9/$3.99
_LONE STAR AND THE TRAIL OF MURDER #124	0-515-10998-3/$3.99
_LONE STAR AND THE WOLF PACK #125	0-515-11019-1/$3.99
_LONE STAR AND THE CHICAGO SHOWDOWN #126	0-515-11044-2/$3.99
_LONE STAR AND THE BRUTUS GANG #127 (March 1993)	0-515-11062-0/$3.99
_LONE STAR AND THE GOLD MINE #128 (April 1993)	0-515-11083-3/$3.99

For Visa, MasterCard and American Express orders ($15 minimum) call: 1-800-631-8571

Check book(s). Fill out coupon. Send to:
BERKLEY PUBLISHING GROUP
390 Murray Hill Pkwy., Dept. B
East Rutherford, NJ 07073

NAME_____

ADDRESS_____

CITY_____

STATE_____ ZIP _____

PLEASE ALLOW 6 WEEKS FOR DELIVERY.
PRICES ARE SUBJECT TO CHANGE
WITHOUT NOTICE.

POSTAGE AND HANDLING:
$1.75 for one book, 75¢ for each additional. Do not exceed $5.50.

BOOK TOTAL $____

POSTAGE & HANDLING $____

APPLICABLE SALES TAX $____
(CA, NJ, NY, PA)

TOTAL AMOUNT DUE $____

PAYABLE IN US FUNDS.
(No cash orders accepted.)

200e

If you enjoyed this book, subscribe now and get...

TWO FREE

A $7.00 VALUE—

If you would like to read more of the very best, most exciting, adventurous, action-packed Westerns being published today, you'll want to subscribe to True Value's Western Home Subscription Service.

Each month the editors of True Value will select the 6 very best Westerns from America's leading publishers for special readers like you. You'll be able to preview these new titles as soon as they are published, *FREE* for ten days with no obligation!

TWO FREE BOOKS

When you subscribe, we'll send you your first month's shipment of the newest and best 6 Westerns for you to preview. With your first shipment, two of these books will be yours as our introductory gift to you absolutely *FREE* (a $7.00 value), regardless of what you decide to do. If you like them, as much as we think you will, keep all six books but pay for just 4 at the low subscriber rate of just $2.75 each. If you decide to return them, keep 2 of the titles as our gift. No obligation.

Special Subscriber Savings

When you become a True Value subscriber you'll save money several ways. First, all regular monthly selections will be billed at the low subscriber price of just $2.75 each. That's at least a savings of $4.50 each month below the publishers price. Second, there is never any shipping, handling or other hidden charges—*Free home delivery*. What's more there is no minimum number of books you must buy, you may return any selection for full credit and you can cancel your subscription at any time. A TRUE VALUE!

A special offer for people who enjoy reading the best Westerns published today.

WESTERNS!

NO OBLIGATION

Mail the coupon below

To start your subscription and receive 2 FREE WESTERNS, fill out the coupon below and mail it today. We'll send your first shipment which includes 2 FREE BOOKS as soon as we receive it.

Mail To: **True Value Home Subscription Services, Inc. P.O. Box 5235
120 Brighton Road, Clifton, New Jersey 07015-5235**

YES! I want to start reviewing the very best Westerns being published today. Send me my first shipment of 6 Westerns for me to preview FREE for 10 days. If I decide to keep them, I'll pay for just 4 of the books at the low subscriber price of $2.75 each; a total $11.00 (a $21.00 value). Then each month I'll receive the 6 newest and best Westerns to preview Free for 10 days. If I'm not satisfied I may return them within 10 days and owe nothing. Otherwise I'll be billed at the special low subscriber rate of $2.75 each; a total of $16.50 (at least a $21.00 value) and save $4.50 off the publishers price. There are never any shipping, handling or other hidden charges. I understand I am under no obligation to purchase any number of books and I can cancel my subscription at any time, no questions asked. In any case the 2 FREE books are mine to keep.

Name _____

Street Address _____ Apt. No. _____

City _____ State _____ Zip Code _____

Telephone _____

Signature _____
(if under 18 parent or guardian must sign)

Terms and prices subject to change. Orders subject to acceptance by True Value Home Subscription Services, Inc.

11044

Classic Westerns from
GILES TIPPETTE

Justa Williams is a bold young Texan who doesn't usually set out looking for trouble...but somehow he always seems to find it.

__JAILBREAK 0-515-10595-3/$3.95
Justa gets a telegram saying there are squatters camped on the Half-Moon ranch, near the Mexican border. Justa's brother, Norris, gets in a whole heap of trouble when he decides to investigate.

__HARD ROCK 0-515-10731-X/$3.99
Justa Williams and his brothers have worked too hard to lose what's taken a lifetime to build. Now the future of the ranch may depend on a bankrupt granger who's offering his herd of six hundred cattle at rock-bottom price. To Justa, a deal this good is a deal too risky....

__SIXKILLER 0-515-10846-4/$4.50
Springtime on the Half-Moon ranch has never been so hard. On top of running the biggest spread in Matagorda County, Justa is about to become a daddy. Which means he's got a lot more to fight for when Sam Sixkiller comes to town.

__GUNPOINT 0-515-10952-5/$4.50
No man tells Justa Williams what to do with his money—at gunpoint or otherwise...until crooked cattleman J.C. Flood hits upon a scheme to bleed the Half-Moon Ranch dry—and Justa's prize cattle and quarterhorses start dying....

For Visa, MasterCard and American Express orders ($15 minimum) call: 1-800-631-8571

FOR MAIL ORDERS: CHECK BOOK(S). FILL OUT COUPON. SEND TO:	**POSTAGE AND HANDLING:** $1.75 for one book, 75¢ for each additional. Do not exceed $5.50.
BERKLEY PUBLISHING GROUP 390 Murray Hill Pkwy., Dept. B East Rutherford, NJ 07073	**BOOK TOTAL** $ ____
NAME_____	**POSTAGE & HANDLING** $ ____
ADDRESS _____	**APPLICABLE SALES TAX** $ ____ (CA, NJ, NY, PA)
CITY_____	**TOTAL AMOUNT DUE** $ ____
STATE_____ ZIP_____	**PAYABLE IN US FUNDS.** (No cash orders accepted.)
PLEASE ALLOW 6 WEEKS FOR DELIVERY. PRICES ARE SUBJECT TO CHANGE WITHOUT NOTICE.	